SOOTHE THE BURN

SOOTHE THE BURN

...Alvix's fingers fumbled at the buttons at Cooper's groin. As much as he wanted to touch all of Cooper's dark, smooth body, he wanted to feel the man's prick in his mouth. It was a burning desire to drink Cooper's seed, tasting the familiar salty bitterness of cum flavored with Cooper's own special essence.

Cooper shivered as the cool night air hit his hard cock when Alvix revealed it to the darkness. Alvix hummed and ran his finger down the length of it.

"Very pretty," he murmured.

A choked laugh came from Cooper. "Will you think it's pretty when it's like the rest of me?"

"Well, considering I get hard the moment I see you, I don't think you have anything to worry about in that department." He fisted Cooper's shaft and pumped.

"Ah." Cooper arched off the ground.

Alvix pushed the top blanket off them and slid down to sprawl between Cooper's spread thighs. He licked the spongy head of Cooper's cock, letting the man's pre-cum coat his tongue. He kept stroking with one hand, while fondling Cooper's heavy balls in the other hand. His own erection pressed against the stiff fabric of his pants, informing Alvix it wouldn't be long after Cooper came that Alvix would spill his seed as well.

Saliva pooled in his mouth as he swallowed Cooper down, taking as much of his cock as he could until the head hit the back of his throat. For the first time, his non-existent gag reflex made him happy...

SOOTHE THE BURN

BY

T. A. CHASE

AMBER QUILL PRESS, LLC
http://www.amberquill.com

SOOTHE THE BURN
AN AMBER QUILL PRESS BOOK

Amber Quill Press, LLC
http://www.amberquill.com

Layout and Formatting provided by: ElementalAlchemy.com

PUBLISHED IN THE UNITED STATES OF AMERICA

Thank you to all my readers.
I appreciate every email you've sent me about how
you love my stories. Sharing them with you is what
keeps me going. C, I love you as always.

CHAPTER 1

Alvix shot to his feet and kicked the side of his ship. "Fucking piece of shit. You would pick this port to puke in."

He shifted slightly. God, he needed to get off Space Port 2456 before the security chief informed Weldon he was there. He kicked his transport ship again, but with less force this time. It wasn't the old girl's fault he'd had to jury rig so many of her parts. He didn't have a lot of extra cash, and Weldon's reach extended farther in the galaxy than Alvix first thought.

"Probably should've stayed and tried to pay off that debt," he muttered as he knelt down to tweak one of the bolts.

Being one of Weldon's playthings for the rest of his life had been his only option besides running. There wasn't any way he could deal with Weldon's perversions any longer.

"Damn." He sucked on his scraped knuckle.

"I might be able to help."

Alvix shot to his feet and whirled, holding the wrench as a weapon. *Getting careless, Alvix.*

The man standing in front of him looked more machine than human. Silver eyes studied him. At least, he assumed they were looking at him. With no defined pupil or iris, just a pure field of silver, it was hard to figure out where the man was looking.

Dark metal covered the stranger's entire face and both arms. Alvix assumed there was more steel under the black vest and pants covering his body.

"Would you like me to look at your ship for you?" The stranger gestured to Alvix's wrench. "You seem to be at an impasse."

"A what?" He frowned.

"An impasse. A situation from which there is no escape," the man explained.

"Ah. Do you know anything about ionic drives?" Alvix asked, handing over the wrench.

"I know a little about them." The odd metal man took the wrench and Alvix's hand in his. "My name is Cooper."

He didn't offer his name. For all he knew, Cooper worked for Weldon and was just waiting for the right moment to take Alvix down. He jerked his hand away when he realized how long they'd been holding hands.

Snorting silently, Alvix shook his head. *What an idiot.* Cooper could snap him in half without breaking a sweat. He averted his eyes as Cooper squatted down next to the drive panel and that black fabric pulled taut over the man's ass.

Not looking. He refrained from slapping himself in the forehead. Looking at some man's ass had gotten the shit beaten out of him a couple weeks ago on one of the Outer System planets. Alvix should have known better. Most places were willing to overlook a man's personal tastes as long as he had the money to pay. He had neither.

When he got caught checking out some miner's butt, the man and his friends took exception and kicked the stuffing out of him. Luckily, they weren't interested in killing him, though it felt like he was dying while he healed.

"Here's your problem." Cooper tapped the wrench against one of the tubes in the compartment. "The main co-axle line leading from the sub-ionic hydraulic drive to the sonic conductor has become obstructed."

"Huh?"

"This line is plugged." Cooper gestured to the tube again.

"Why didn't you just say that?" Irritation sparked in Alvix.

It didn't sound like a quick fix. *Fuck.* He'd already stayed on the port too long. Weldon had to know he was here by now.

"Can you fix it?"

Not that he had any cash to pay the man.

"Yes. It'll take an hour or so. I have to make sure nothing has been compromised because of this." Cooper turned to face him.

"How much is it going to cost me?" His hands twitched and his survival instincts pinged. Weldon was close. Alvix could sense the bastard. Sweat beaded on his forehead as heat raced along his veins.

Cooper tilted his head, and Alvix had the feeling the man was scanning him for something. A look of comprehension crossed Cooper's face.

"It won't cost you anything except transportation."

"Transportation?"

Alvix's breathing sped up. He had to get control of himself or he'd end up doing something he'd regret, like catching his clothes on fire. A cool touch on his cheek shocked him. Cooper caressed his skin, soothing the fire building in his body with the smoothness of his metal surface.

"Yes. I need transportation for me and two others to rendezvous with three of my friends."

His mind cleared enough to notice that Cooper's voice held no emotion or inflection. Alvix heard cyborg soldiers speak the same way. Dispassionate and aloof. The fucking world could be exploding around them and they were unflappable.

Cooper didn't give off the same vibes as cyborgs. Alvix had run into his share of those beings and his senses would have recognized one.

"Where would this rendezvous take place?"

It paid to be suspicious. Going to certain places in the universe signed your death warrant, not only from the Galactic Military, but from the scary things that lived in those places.

Something slimy slithered over his brain, causing him to shiver. It wouldn't be long until Weldon arrived and completely fucked up Alvix's day.

"We only need transportation and we can pay you for your time." Cooper dropped his hand and stepped away.

Darkness threatened to swallow Alvix's mind and he fought against it. He was mentally stronger than any of Weldon's men, which was the reason he'd managed to escape the first time.

"Well...well. I must say I was surprised when Monty informed me you had landed."

Alvix tensed and turned, refusing to allow his fear to show in his eyes. "What do you want, Weldon?"

"Simply what you owe me, Alvix. Twelve thousand dollars for that little drug bill your friend ran up." Weldon's squinty pig eyes remained on him.

Where had Cooper gone? Or was Weldon so intent on taking him that he was willing to ignore the large steel man standing behind Alvix?

"I'll get you your money. I don't have it on me." Alvix smiled. "It's on Space Port 2549. I can be there and back in a week's time."

Weldon's laugh was more like the braying of a donkey. "I'm not stupid. I let you go, you're not coming back. You got away from me once and I don't plan on letting you escape again." The fat man waddled closer, invading Alvix's personal space without concern.

Gritting his teeth, Alvix didn't jerk away when Weldon touched him. Greed, pain, and lust threaded their way through Alvix's nerves. The man's soul was as black and empty as the far reaches of the universe.

"No, I won't let you go, bright one, but I'm willing to let you pay your debt in some other way."

Alvix stumbled away before Weldon's fat lips could touch him.

"I told you before, Weldon, I won't do that. Not anymore. No way in hell." He shot a glance around. *Where did the screwdriver go?*

"So passionate. I'll enjoy taming that fire."

Waving imperiously, Weldon gestured to the two men with him to grab Alvix. This was it. Alvix was dead because there was no way he'd let Weldon take him. He crouched, raising his fists. He'd die fighting.

"Captain Alvix has your money. What account would you like it transferred into?" Cooper's voice broke the tension.

Weldon's goons stopped, then their eyes widened as Cooper came to stand next to Alvix.

"Really? Who might you be?" Weldon still sounded brave.

"I'm Captain Alvix's client. I can have the money I'm paying him for this job transferred into your account. You won't have to worry about his debt anymore."

Alvix didn't relax. Cooper's intervention was great, but Alvix still didn't want to take him and his men anywhere.

"And what if I say no? I happen to be interested in finding an alternate form of payment from Alvix," Weldon challenged Cooper.

"Are you serious about issuing that brave a statement to me? Do you think your men can retrieve Alvix from me if I don't want him to leave?"

Goose bumps rose on Alvix's skin. Somehow, Cooper's questions seemed scarier, without any emotion in them, than Weldon's arrogant sputtering.

"You're only one man, no matter how much metal you have

4

attached to your body." Weldon pointed to Alvix. "Fetch him here."

Alvix bristled at sounding like an object Cooper and Weldon were fighting over. He reset his feet because he wasn't giving up without a fight.

"Who said I was the only one?"

"Looks like you've got a bit of trouble, LT. May we be of assistance?" Another unemotional voice drifted into the conversation from behind Weldon.

Alvix looked beyond Weldon to the two men standing behind the other man. *Holy fucking shit.* There was a freaking army of metal men wandering around the spaceport.

"Damn. How many are there of you steel men?" He shot a look at Cooper.

"There are six of us altogether. That is why I hired you to transport us to where the others are." Cooper didn't look at him. Those silver eyes remained focused on Weldon and his men.

"Oh." Alvix had a sinking feeling he would be flying to wherever these men wanted to go.

"If you will give the staff sergeant your account number, we'll have the money in there within ten minutes." Cooper nodded toward the enormous, dark-skinned soldier stepping up beside Weldon.

Weldon glared at Alvix while handing over his bankcard. "I won't forget this, Alvix. I'll still have you. Remember that."

As much as Alvix wanted to make a smart-ass comment, he knew better. He acknowledged the warning, knowing Weldon would be waiting for a careless moment.

Silence reigned until after Weldon and his men left. It was then that Alvix realized three large strangers surrounded him.

"Ummm…if you want to head out, we need to get supplies, and you'll need to fix the thingie." He gestured in the direction of the drive.

"LT?"

Somehow, from the tilt of the sergeant's head, Alvix understood the man was questioning Alvix's seeming lack of respect.

"You and Callum ordered our supplies, right?" Cooper pulled the wrench from where he had stuck it in his waistband at the small of his back.

"Yes." Callum joined them. His eyes were solid blue. "They'll be delivered within the hour."

"Good. Rivers, you'll help me. Alvix, you need to show Callum where we can put our supplies when they arrive." Cooper's orders were brisk and concise.

"Yes, sir." Callum turned to Alvix. "Where's your cargo hold?"

"In there." He jerked a thumb over his shoulder at the entrance door to his ship. "I'm sure you can find it. I have something to do since we'll be here for another hour."

"No."

He laughed. "I appreciate you paying me for a trip I don't really want to take, but I'm not one of your men."

Alvix went inside the ship, grabbed a small bag, and headed out.

*   *   *

Cooper and his men watched their ship's captain saunter away.

"LT?" Callum sounded unsure.

"Follow him. Don't let him see you, though. Don't interfere, but make sure Weldon's men stay away from him."

"All right." Callum saluted and left.

"Why don't we just take his ship? Let that fat slug have him." Rivers knelt down and unscrewed one end of the plugged tube.

"After what was taken from us, you want to take from someone else?" Cooper stroked a hand over his metal jaw as he thought about the slender blond pilot.

Rivers grunted. "We agreed to the experiment, Cooper. We might not have understood all of the consequences, but we signed the papers." He yanked the tube out.

Cooper took it and studied it. "Too blocked. We need a new one."

"He's not going to take us to Tongass. Once he knows where we're going, he'll freak out, and we'll end up having to take his ship anyway." Rivers kept talking, even though Cooper wasn't responding to him.

"Here." Cooper handed over a clean tube he'd dug out of a small box of repair items.

When Rivers grabbed it, Cooper didn't let it go until his friend met his gaze. "It'll work out, Rivers, even if we have to find a different ship. I'd prefer we didn't, but we don't have a choice. Our teammates are counting on us to come get them."

Rivers' sigh didn't sound convinced, but Cooper didn't care. Their mission was so important he couldn't allow any doubts or obstacles to deter them.

"Who is this guy? When General Gateway came up with this crazy rescue plan, he mentioned a couple of transport pilots to fly the rescue mission, and you jumped on this guy. Do you know him from somewhere?"

He didn't want to talk about it really, but Rivers had been one of his closest friends since basic training. "Remember our first post on Raspion?"

"Yeah." Rivers shivered. "That was a nasty planet."

Nodding, Cooper let Rivers take the new tube and start fitting it in the drive. "I used to go into the town closest to base, just for a change of scenery. There was this tall, skinny kid who worked one of the corners near a bar I frequented."

"Worked? He sell himself?" Rivers' back muscles flexed as he tightened the bolt.

"Not that I know of. He was a pickpocket. Pretty good one from what I saw. That town was full of thieves, mercs, and all around bad men, but the kid never got caught as far as I know." Cooper rested against the side of the ship.

Rivers wiped his hands on his pants and stood. "Why do you remember him?"

Leaning his head back, Cooper closed his eyes and shrugged. "Don't know. Guess there was something inside me that said if I hadn't gone into the military, I could've been that kid."

Rivers started checking the rest of the engine. "You ever talk to him?"

"I bought him a meal once. It was during one of those monsoons that hit Raspion so often. Kid was standing on the corner, drenched, but I just knew he hadn't met his quota or whatever and couldn't go back to wherever he lived. When I approached him, he probably thought I was going to proposition him, and I could see him weighing the possibilities." He chuckled. "He was shocked when I offered to buy him some food. We ate, didn't talk or share names, nothing personal like that. I left first, but not before leaving a pile of credits on the table. I just wanted him to get out of the cold."

He ducked his head and kept his eyes closed. He didn't want to see the knowing look gracing Rivers' face at the moment. He was a sucker for a tough luck story. He helped out when other soldiers' families needed things.

"How did you know it was this particular kid the general had on the list?" Rivers shut the engine hood with a snap.

"I asked around after not seeing him for a couple of days. Someone told me his name was Alvix. Before I could do anything except ask, we were transferred off that planet and I pushed him to the back of my mind, though every once in a while, I wondered what he was up to."

"Guess you found out." Rivers snorted.

"Guess so. Let's check out the rest of the ship and make sure it's trip worthy. We'll worry later about convincing him to take us."

Rivers stepped into the ship, and Cooper followed, trying not to worry about Alvix's reaction when he found out where they wanted him to take them.

CHAPTER 2

Tension easing, Alvix stepped onto the dock where his ship was anchored. Going out into the town wasn't a good idea when Weldon was still angry about not getting a hold of him. He'd avoided three mercs trying to grab him and one of the metal men took out two others while Alvix got away. Good thing the lieutenant had someone follow him.

"Finish your errand?"

He jerked and whirled to find the very man he'd been thinking of standing in the shadows, arms crossed and looming menacingly.

"Yeah. I did. Thanks." Alvix motioned to the engine. "Did you get her fixed?"

"Of course. If I didn't, we wouldn't be able to leave."

Rolling his eyes mentally, Alvix hoped their trip wouldn't take long. Dealing with the man's arrogance might lead to him getting his ass kicked because he couldn't keep his mouth shut.

The blue-eyed soldier, Callum, strolled up a minute later. "LT, the supplies are here."

"Get Rivers and help them load the ship. Captain Alvix and I are going to the bridge to get the ship ready to fly."

"Yes, sir."

Callum saluted again, while Rivers stepped from Alvix's ship and grabbed one of the long boxes being hauled by a hover cart.

Alvix didn't want to go with Cooper, but didn't see any way out of doing what the man wanted. He followed Cooper into his ship, frowning as a memory tried to surface. Whatever his brain was trying to tell him wasn't willing to come out at the moment, so he pushed it aside. It would come to him eventually.

They entered the bridge, and he sat in the pilot seat.

"Why are you metal?" He winced and decided he had to learn how not to say everything that came into his head.

Cooper eyed him. It might have been a rude question, but Alvix wasn't going to make this stupid trip afraid of what the man might do to him.

"All of my skin has been replaced with flexible titanium sheets."

"Seriously? Even…" He shot a surreptitious glance at Cooper's groin.

"Yes, even the skin there. Don't worry. It's fully functioning."

The cold amusement in Cooper's voice caused Alvix to blush. *Shit.* His interest must have been more obvious than he thought.

"You'll need to enter the coordinates since I have no clue where you want us to go."

"We are going to Tongass, Captain."

"Fuck." Alvix clenched his hands and fought the fear rising in his chest. "You're kidding, right? The Galactic Military declared it too dangerous even for their soldiers."

"We fought a war with the inhabitants of that planet. Hundreds of thousands of soldiers died there." Cooper typed the coordinates into Alvix's navigation system. "Three of our team mates were left behind, and we're going back to rescue them."

"Are you crazy?"

The soldier pinned him with empty silver eyes, and Alvix realized he didn't want to know the answer to that question.

"No man left behind is our motto." Cooper's gaze trailed over Alvix, leaving goose bumps in its wake. "Do you understand the concept of such loyalty?"

Alvix shook his head, fiddling with the knobs on the nav system while avoiding Cooper's gaze. "Nope. Been left behind too many times to believe in that crap anymore."

Cooper growled, though it sounded more like two gears grinding together than human.

"Don't get me wrong, man." Alvix held up a hand to keep Cooper from responding. "You believe in it and since you're paying me for my services, I'll keep my opinions to myself."

He said the words and meant them, though in a hidden, not yet hardened part of his soul, he wished someone cared enough about him to come back for him. "Are we ready to take off?" The flight plans uploaded, he wanted to get to Tongass and back before the GalMil came after them.

Cooper tapped the side of his head, and Alvix checked closer to see there was a device imbedded in the man's ear.

"My men are aboard with our supplies. We're ready to depart whenever you are, Captain."

Alvix snorted. "Captain? As you can tell, I'm not very formal, so you can call me Alvix. Sit down and strap in. You do know we'll be dodging GalMil ships as well as the Tongassians once we're out of hyper-drive."

"Get us to those coordinates, Alvix. My men and I will do the rest."

"Yes, sir."

He tightened his web harness and focused on the screens in front of him. He wasn't aware of Cooper's approach until the man leaned over his shoulder.

"You may call me Cooper," he whispered into Alvix's ear.

Holy Christ. Alvix's heart skipped a beat and his cock took a great deal of interest in how arousing he found the intermingled scents of man and oil.

"Umm…okay. Sure, Cooper," he stuttered. "You should sit. I can't take off until you're secure."

*   *   *

Cooper took a seat to the right and slightly behind Alvix. It gave him a clear view of all the computer screens, so he could keep an eye on the man and make sure he didn't change the coordinates.

::The kid has the hots for you, LT.:: Callum MacDonald's amused voice chirped in Cooper's ear.

Cooper cringed and turned down the volume. He was still getting used to the upgrades he'd gone through before his team headed out on this mission. He flipped up the screen on his left wrist and typed something in to make it look like he was working. The internal link among all the members of his team sparked through his brain. That way they could communicate without Alvix knowing they were talking about him.

::We don't have time for distracts, Callum. We left Tongass over a week ago. Time is running out for Steele, Apple, and Pope.::

11

::We understand that, LT...just trying to lighten things up.::

He rubbed his face, grimacing at the cool surface of his cheek under his hand. *::Sorry. Where did our pilot go while Rivers and I fixed his ship?::*

::He dropped a small package off to some old woman. Didn't seem illegal or anything. I saved his ass from a couple of mercs, but he can handle himself as long as he's not attacked by more than one guy.::

::Thank you, Callum. Now if we can get the others back, we should be in good shape again.:: It was hard not having his entire team together.

::LT, you do realize the probability of them being alive is about twenty percent. If they were captured by the Tongassians, they're more than likely dead.:: His ever practical staff sergeant, Rivers, joined the conversation.

::I know, but we have to try. They would come back for us.::

The silence greeting his statement told him all he needed to know. He was the commander of the most elite unit of soldiers in the GalMil. They were the unit who never questioned orders and the men who allowed their lives to become nothing but pawns for their superiors, even to the point of becoming metal monsters.

Yet the break for Cooper came three weeks ago when they went to Tongass with orders to assassinate the ruling family over all his protests. Killing soldiers and men who fought back was one thing and a job he could accept. Killing women and children went beyond Cooper's personal code of ethics. He wouldn't kill innocents.

He'd lodged a formal complaint, but their orders weren't changed and they inserted onto Tongass.

::Someone screwed us.:: Cooper finally admitted the words churning in all of their guts since they were extracted a week ago.

::The quality of soldiers is getting worse, LT. Even the support people are sub-par. I don't think they did it on purpose.:: Rivers' thoughts were more a growl.

::Somehow they only allowed enough time for three of us to get to the evac site. The logistics person didn't take into consideration the time needed in case we were retreating under fire,:: Callum pointed out.

::Shit. Not only do we have to rescue them from a planet of fire-breathing men, we have to figure out who fucked up the evacuation.:: He sighed. *::It was so much easier when we knew who the enemy was.::*

::Roger that, LT.::

12

"Cooper?"

He flipped the screen closed and met Alvix's curious light green eyes with his own blank ones. "Yes?"

"Why are you like that?" Alvix waved a hand at Cooper's left side. "Were you burned or injured?"

::No, just stupid.:: His mind link sent his thoughts to Rivers and Callum. He'd forgotten about that other little improvement as well.

::Amen, LT,:: both men replied.

"It's highly classified. My men and I were chosen to test an advanced type of armor."

It was more than armor. With the nano-mites used to create the titanium, the armor had become a living part of Cooper's body. He was literally becoming a man of steel. It could heal almost any damage, but the scariest part was when any part of Cooper's real flesh was injured, the nano-mites would gather around the wound, heal it, and another part of Cooper became titanium. His unit was the elite of the GalMil so they went into the most dangerous situations and within a year, the titanium armor completely covered them.

He feared that eventually he would no longer be human. In his darkest nightmares, Cooper was an emotionless robot, killing without question and loving no one.

"That's a creepy experiment, man." Alvix shuddered before turning back to his bank of computers. "We got clearance for take-off. Strap in and hold on. When we drop out of hyper-drive, I'll be hauling ass to get us to the surface before we're shot down by GalMil ships or attacked by whatever the Tongassians have."

"They have fire-breathing creatures that fly," Cooper muttered.

"Seriously?" Alvix gave him a wild-eyed glance.

"Yes, seriously."

"God above, what the hell have you gotten me into? I'm starting to think being Weldon's play toy would've been better than this shit."

The image of Alvix on his knees, sucking Cooper's cock flashed into Cooper's mind so quickly, he wasn't able to block it from the others.

::See, I told you he was cute.:: Callum snickered.

"Quiet."

Alvix jerked at Cooper's barked order. Cooper didn't feel like explaining he was talking to one of his men and not Alvix.

"Again, Alvix, just get us there. We'll take care of the rest."

"Yes, sir."

*   *   *

Dropping out of hyper drive was like having his stomach suddenly plunge to the soles of his feet. Alvix ignored the resulting nausea and headed immediately toward the surface of Tongass. There weren't any GalMil ships showing up on radar, but it didn't mean anything. They could show up at any moment.

"We'll be landing at the coordinates in fifteen minutes, Cooper. You and your men should get ready."

Cooper grunted and stood. He dropped a heavy hand on Alvix's shoulder as he went by to the elevator that would take him down to the cargo hold of Alvix's ship.

Was it an incidental touch? Had Cooper meant to grab the back of Alvix's chair and got him instead?

The hard squeeze Cooper administered made Alvix wince, even as it cleared up the questions in his mind.

His ship shuddered as it entered Tongass's atmosphere. *Get your brain back on flying.* Alvix could only hope his small ship wouldn't create a blip on anyone's radar screen.

Flying creatures that breathed fire? He shook his head. The love/hate relationship he had with destructive flames didn't tempt him to search out one of those beings. Were they even real? Or just an intricate machine?

As they hovered over the site, he hit the intercom to the loading dock. "Cooper, I'm setting her down. You ready to off load?"

That probably wasn't proper military language, but since Cooper and his men were the closest to the military Alvix had ever been, he doubted they would bother him about it.

"Yes, we're ready. After we're off, get out of here. You should be able to hide behind the planet's moon. I'll radio you when we need to be picked up."

"Okay."

He turned off the intercom and swore. No fucking way did he want to hang around this part of the universe. The GalMil had declared this quadrant off limits to every kind of space travel except sanctioned military ops, and Alvix had the feeling Cooper didn't have permission to be on this planet.

Alvix touched down as softly as a butterfly on a flower. He opened the intercom while lowering the ramp. "We're down."

"And we're out." Cooper hesitated. "Get away from here, Alvix. I'll ping you when we're ready for you to come get us."

"All right. I still think you're crazy, man."

"It's possible." A pause before Cooper cleared his throat. "We met before."

Alvix stared at the intercom. "We did?"

"Yes. Of course, I looked a lot different back then. It was on Raspion."

Wait. He closed his eyes and thought about those months before he ended up on Space Port 2456 and Weldon's control. He remembered a good-looking soldier who bought him a meal and left a wad of cash on the table for him. "That was you?"

"You disappeared after that, and I got transferred before I could find you."

"LT, we have to go." One of his fellow soldiers' voices drifted over the intercom.

"Get out of here, Alvix, and we'll see you on the other side."

"Roger. Take care of yourself, Cooper."

He ended the communication, not sure why he felt like he was never going to see the man again and why that thought bothered him so much.

Turning on the outside camera, he watched as Cooper and his two men slipped into the trees surrounding the clearing he'd landed in.

"Mission started," he muttered and shook his head.

His fear of Weldon and what the man would do to him put him on the course he was currently on, ending up on a hostile planet, playing pick-up man for a doomed rescue mission.

Alvix thumped the back of his head on the chair behind him. How did he manage to get himself into situations like this? God, it was like a gift or something. He would get himself into trouble and there was never anyone to bail him out. He stared at the spot where the three men had disappeared into the forest.

What would it be like to have friends like Cooper and the other two? Friends he could count on to come and save his ass, even if it was a suicide mission.

Grimacing, Alvix started the lift-off sequence. He'd never know that kind of friendship. By the time he was sixteen, anyone remotely close to him had abandoned him. People didn't like him for some reason. Probably knew he was fucked up inside and didn't want any of the shit rubbing off on them.

He plotted a course to a spot behind the Tongassian moon, hoping Cooper was right about hiding out there. So far, the Tongassians hadn't left their planet, so he only had to worry about the GalMil finding him.

After an uneventful lift-off, Alvix headed for space. He wiped away the sweat beading on his forehead. The air cooling system must be on the fritz again. He'd check it out when he got settled. The air grew hot and heavy, constricting his lungs until black dots spiraled before his eyes. His body absorbed as much of the heat as it could, but he'd never been overwhelmed by fire before. What was happening?

Panic gripped him and he clamped onto the armrests of his chair. As his world exploded around him, he hoped Cooper would forgive him for not coming back.

CHAPTER 3

"Move, human."

A burning spike drove into Cooper's lower back, drawing a pained hiss from him. *Shit.* By the time the Tongassians killed him, he'd be all titanium at the rate he was being injured. He could feel the nano-mites crawling through his blood stream and under his flesh, searching out each injury and healing it in their own bizarre way.

"Quit pushing. I'm going as fast as you'll let me. Take off these cuffs and I could move even faster."

Cooper dipped his head, hiding his smile. Callum was all right, cranky and pissed about the Tongassians capturing them, but he hadn't sustained the injuries Cooper and Rivers had.

The only way Cooper knew Rivers was still with them was the steady beat of the staff sergeant's heart in Cooper's ear. All their vitals linked through monitors in each of their brains. It was how he knew Steele, Apple, and Pope were still alive. The moment they stepped onto the planet, their vitals appeared, though Pope's was fading and that scared Cooper.

Of course, none of it mattered any more. They would all be dead soon. He bit his lip clear through as another fiery spike slammed into his hip.

At least his team would die like they'd lived most of their lives. Since Basic, they'd been training, fighting, and living together. Cooper admitted to himself that he'd always hoped they would die together.

::We're with you, LT.:: Rivers' words danced through his mind.

::Side by side,:: Callum chimed in.

::Blood for blood.:: Steele spoke for the first time.

::Watching each other's back.:: He finished their team creed.

Alvix flashed through his mind. Cooper hoped the pilot made it off planet and wouldn't wait around for them too long.

"Kneel."

A solid blow to his knees dropped him to the floor. Keeping his head lowered, he studied his surroundings.

They were in a large room filled with Tongassians. Cooper remembered the first time he'd ever seen one of the aliens. One of the regular GalMil units had managed to capture it. There was no way to tell whether it was male or female. At eight feet tall, the Tongassian towered over the soldiers and it looked like a solid pillar of flame. Orange, red, and at the heart of the creature, blue.

Cooper knew blue flames were the hottest and burned the most pure, so he assumed that was where the Tongassian's heart lay. Constructed out of fire, their mere touch could give a man third-degree burns. They threw fireballs and sticks as well. They had no reason to get in close with GalMil soldiers. Their powers allowed them to kill from afar. Hence, the thousands of soldiers killed on the planet during the war.

The room stifled Cooper, heating his titanium skin to red-hot metal, but it wouldn't melt or warp. Something within the nano-mites absorbed the heat until it reached a bearable level.

"Have you come to finish your mission?"

He raised his head slightly to spy the platform in front of him. A Tongassian sat on an obsidian throne, a crown of blue flames wreathing its head. This must be the king.

::Yeah, LT. He's a nasty bastard. Be careful with him.:: Steele's voice rang into his ear.

::Steele, how are you? Report.::

::We're fucked, LT. Ain't no way out of this. Apple and me, we're okay, but that Tongassian bastard's been doing some shit to Pope and he's in a bad way.::

Not Pope. The youngest and best of them, Pope was on the fast track to becoming a Supreme General in the GalMil, if he survived his time in Cooper's unit first. Cooper and the others knew who Pope was and who his father was, but they never treated the young soldier any differently. Pope never asked for special treatment. Cooper could only hope Pope got a posthumous medal when the news got out about his death.

Scorching heat blinded Cooper as his guard hit him on the back of the head. "Answer His Majesty."

Blinking, trying to get his eyes back to normal, Cooper shook his head. "No, Your Majesty. I returned to take my men back home."

"Hmm...how do I know you're telling the truth?" The king tilted his head. "You could just be saying that to get close to me."

"Sire, you can kill us from where you sit. Why would I risk our lives to kill you? I knew the futility of the mission, yet I'm a mere soldier and must follow orders."

Scraping and shuffling drew his attention away from the king. Steele and Apple were escorted in, Pope supported between them. Cooper swallowed the curse threatening to burst from him.

Pope must have suffered so much damage that the nano-mites were overloaded. Titanium covered only two-thirds of the young soldier's body. The rest of his flesh was black and charred by flame. He looked like he'd stood in the middle of a fire. Being the newest member of the unit, Pope had only received one round of injections, so he still had some skin on his body. At least, he did before the Tongassian king had gotten to him.

"Pretty words, human. I must thank you and your military for sending me such a delicious play toy. The fire looks so beautiful dancing along his flesh."

Horror-stricken, Cooper could only watch as the king pointed at Pope and the man burst into flame. All the metal flashed white-hot and the flesh blackened even more. Pope threw his head back, but no scream emanated from his destroyed throat. Yet Cooper pressed his fists to his ears, moaning at the anguish ripping through their internal link.

"Stop."

Everyone froze, and Cooper figured no one had ever told the king to do anything. The fire disappeared like it never was, and Pope crumbled to the floor, his body so damaged, he couldn't even shudder.

A struggle happened behind Cooper and then footsteps flew past him. His mouth dropped open when he saw Alvix standing before the Tongassian king.

"Where did this creature come from?" The ruler seemed to glare at the guards.

"He was on the human ship we captured, sire. We assumed he had something to do with the soldiers and you would wish to deal with them all together." One of the guards dropped to his knees.

The king gestured and the guard crawled away as the ruler's attention landed on Alvix. Alvix trembled and sweat popped up on his forehead. Something was happening, and Cooper wondered what was going on.

Alvix gasped and exploded into flame. Cooper was on his feet and moving before his guard could stop him.

"Alvix," he yelled, not sure if the man could hear him over the rushing fire.

Alvix opened his eyes and shook his head. "Don't touch me."

"How can I help you?"

"You can't." Alvix squinted past Cooper to where the Tongassian ruler sat, watching all of their interaction with interest.

::But I might be able to save you.::

Cooper jerked as Alvix's voice joined the others in his head.

::How?::

Alvix tilted his head to where Pope lay, surround by Rivers and the others. *::We're linked. The young soldier, Pope, will always have fire in his soul now. I have an affinity for fire.::*

::How can you save us?::

A mental shake of the head. *::Don't have a concrete plan. Whatever I decide, don't say anything. Don't argue. Just get the fuck out of here.::*

The link faded as the blaze around Alvix died. Cooper fought the guard dragging him away. The flesh on his right arm sizzled and he moaned.

"Cower with your pathetic men."

Cooper slammed into the cool marble floor, unable to catch himself because of the pain.

"Who is that?" Steele mumbled under his breath while helping Cooper sit up.

"He's the pilot who flew us here."

He didn't take his eyes off what was happening on the platform. Although Alvix had been lit up like an old-fashion Earth firework, there were no burns anywhere. The only things affected by the flames had been Alvix's clothes, leaving the pilot naked and shivering.

The vulnerable curve of the slender pilot's ass tempted Cooper. He jerked his gaze away, only to find all eyes seemed to be on Alvix. Cooper wished he had a shirt or something to cover him with. It had to be degrading in some way, though why was Cooper worried about that?

"Well, what have you brought me, human? Maybe we can work out a trade."

The king stood and strolled to Alvix. Reaching out, he drew a finger down the center of Alvix's chest, carving a red line of abused skin. Alvix twitched, but didn't say a word.

Alvix drew a breath only after the Tongassian returned to his throne. Cooper had no idea what Alvix was about to say, but he had a feeling he wasn't going to like it.

"You let all of them go free, take my ship, and leave your planet. I'll stay here and be your plaything."

Cooper started to climb to his feet, his disapproval roaring to get out. Steele and Callum held him down.

::No way, LT. Stay with us and keep your mouth shut.:: Steele's grip on Cooper's arm was like a vise.

Didn't they understand Alvix was sacrificing himself for them? That was way more than he'd asked for when he helped Alvix back at the space port.

::LT.::

He whirled to look at Pope, whose eyes were closed and his breathing ragged. Were the nano-mites turning his lungs into titanium or had they been that damaged by the fire?

"Pope, how's it going, kid?"

"Fucking sucks, sir."

"I imagine."

Pope might have flinched as he shifted. It was hard to tell because of all the injuries he'd suffered. *::The man's right, LT. He's our best chance to get off this god-forsaken planet without any of us dying.::*

::But to give up his own freedom for ours? It's not right. Now when he didn't sign on for it.::

Their conversation took place while Alvix stood, facing the king and sweating at the heat surrounding him.

::No, he didn't sign up for it, but it's his choice, and we have to respect his right to make it.:: Steele grasped his wrist, and Cooper's throat closed.

Cooper understood that the life of one man wasn't more important than the lives of hundreds, but it was hard to accept watching that concept come to life in front of him.

"Why should I agree to that? I have all of you in my power. I could do whatever I want to any of them." The king's smug voice grated over Cooper's nerves.

He steeled himself for pain as the king's gaze trailed over him. Alvix moved, not a lot, but enough to bring the king's attention back to him.

"They are intriguing humans with seemingly unlimited strength, but even they will burn up eventually. Their bodies are fragile and pathetic, not meant for sharing the flames with the fire god. You would go through them too quickly, with no one to glory in your radiance. And it's more fun to have a willing partner."

"What makes you more special than these metal men?" The king sounded skeptical.

"I'm a fire-eater."

At Alvix's announcement, a ripple of surprise wound through the gathered crowd.

What the fuck is a fire-eater? Did being one explain why only Alvix's clothes burned in the Tongassian's fire?

"We believed fire-eaters were mere myths. Legends for us to dream of by our late night fires."

Alvix shrugged. "Don't know anything about your myths, but I'm real and I can take anything you can dish out."

There wasn't a boastful tone to Alvix's words, just sheer confidence.

The king rose and gestured to Alvix. "You will come with me and prove that what you say is true. If I'm satisfied, I will release these men."

Alvix followed the Tongassian without looking back at Cooper, no matter how loudly he begged. Silence fell over the throne room, and Cooper turned to study his men. Of the six of them, it looked like Callum and Steele were the fittest. Both Cooper and Rivers had received injuries when the Tongassians captured them.

Apple didn't look wounded, but there was a wildness to his eyes that Cooper didn't like. He noticed how Callum sat next to Apple, talking to him softly and keeping him grounded. Pope was the worst off. Cooper sat next to the man and let him rest on his shoulder.

"Why you?"

"LT?" Pope fidgeted in pain.

"Why did he do all his flame shit on you? No offense to Apple, but he's skinnier than you and if the point is to inflict as much pain as possible, it would work faster on him."

Pope exhaled raggedly. "He wanted me. This whole mission was about me and my father, I bet. The team was sent here, and I was deliberately captured."

Cooper didn't know where to touch Pope without causing the man pain as coughs wracked his body.

"The asshole told me while he roasted me that he was to inflict as much pain as possible and if he killed me, no big deal. Someone wants to hurt my father and the unit, LT, and the only way they can do that is through me."

"We figured that out, kid. Don't worry. We'll get you home and fuck up whoever did this to you."

His men settled around him, on guard, but letting their bodies heal. It would take more time than they had to recover completely from their wounds. The nano-mites would bring their strength back to normal at least.

Cooper didn't know how much time went by before the king returned to the throne room. Alvix stumbled in his wake, arms wrapped around his stomach and blood trickling down the backs of his thighs.

"God damn fucking sadistic bastard," Cooper shouted when his mind comprehended what the blood meant. He surged to his feet, freezing only when Alvix shook his head at him.

"Take them to the fire-eater's ship. Escort them off planet."

There was no time to talk to Alvix, to protest what the man did to ensure Cooper and his friends safe passage off the Tongassian planet.

"You take Pope, Steele. Callum, stay with Apple. Rivers, take the point."

Cooper lingered at the back of the group, trying desperately to think of a way to save Alvix.

::No looking back, Cooper. Just go and don't feel guilty about leaving me behind. I told you no one ever comes back for me.::

He shut his eyes and vowed, *::I'll be back, Alvix. I'll free you from this fucking hell.::*

As he followed the others, he mapped the corridors of the palace because he knew he'd be back, even if he came on his own.

CHAPTER 4

Alvix stared at the wall of his room. Night had fallen, but he didn't care. He had no idea how long he'd been on Tongass. It didn't matter anyway. There wasn't anyone waiting for him to return and no one cared what happened to him.

He closed his eyes, ignoring the pain throbbing throughout his body. Somehow, he didn't think anything Weldon did would have been nearly as bad as what was happening to him now.

Gods, Alvix hoped Cooper and his fellow soldiers got free of this place because if they didn't and his noble sacrifice was for nothing, he was going to be pissed. For some reason, the thought of the big lieutenant eased Alvix's loneliness. Knowing Cooper had saved him once before on Raspion helped Alvix believe that, just maybe, Cooper would be back to rescue him from this hell.

Shuffling noises came behind him and he scrunched his eyes tighter together, reconstructing in his mind his fantasy home. Beautiful blue grass cordoned off into squares by white fences. Long-legged creatures called horses grazed on the grass under a bright blue sky. So much like the postcard he saw once of a place called Kentucky on Earth, a planet only the rich and powerful could afford to visit now.

More sounds, but he refused to look. There was always a commotion when the king came to play with him.

"Fuck."

Okay, that didn't sound like any Tongassian Alvix had ever heard. Not that many of them spoke to him.

"Grab the man already, LT. We can't keep this quiet for long."

That voice sounded remarkably like Rivers or so Alvix thought since they'd never really talked to each other that much.

As he rolled over, a dark figure knelt at his side and he flinched away from the hand reaching out toward him.

"Alvix."

He blinked, clearing away all the pain and depression clouding his mind. Cooper leaned forward and gave him a better view of the man's face.

Denial shook Alvix's head. "I told you not to come back."

"No man left behind." Cooper grasped his arm and yanked him to his feet. The soldier rose fluidly as well, even though more of his body seemed to be metal.

"I'm not one of your men, Cooper. I'm not worth risking your life for."

"Let me decide that. Now shut up. You can argue with me later." Cooper glanced over his shoulder.

Alvix looked in that direction and spied Rivers keeping watch in the doorway.

"Can you move without help?" Cooper's gaze trailed over his body.

He took a step away from his pallet and almost collapsed to the floor. Cooper caught him up, flung him over one cool metallic shoulder and waved for Rivers to head out.

"Do you know how embarrassed I'd be if I wasn't so freaking exhausted?"

Cooper tapped a hand on Alvix's ass. "Quiet. There's no alarm yet, but I want to get as close to the pick-up zone as possible before someone raises it."

"Then you better start hustling because I think I'm due a visit from His Royal Majesty soon."

"Shit."

Rivers fell in behind them as Cooper headed down the hallway. At the intersection of the corridor, another man stood. Alvix didn't know his name, but recognized him as one of the soldiers Cooper had come to rescue the first time.

"Steele, take the point," Cooper ordered.

Alvix peered around. Cooper carried him over one shoulder with an arm clamped across his thighs to keep him from falling. Should he be freaking out because Cooper's hand was close enough to his naked ass to pinch it?

He grimaced as pain skated down his spine. That part of his anatomy had gotten a work out since he gave up his freedom, and not in a fun "spend all night with a stud" kind of way either.

The flash of black fabric caught his attention and drew his gaze. Why did Cooper wear pants if he was all titanium?

Black pants covered Cooper's ass and legs. There were pockets on each thigh, hiding all kinds of cool gadgets, Alvix bet. A knife sheath was tied to one leg and a holster holding one handgun graced Cooper's other hip.

Thick black boots completed the outfit. Well, almost. Twisting slightly, Alvix checked out the black vest stretched tight across Cooper's back.

Why would they need vests if they were metal? Wouldn't the bullets bounce off them? Maybe they weren't all metal. Maybe the metal bits were more like patches wherever they were shot or knifed.

He giggled at the thought of Cooper looking like a dog with mange. Another quick slap to his ass quieted him, and he smothered his next snicker. Did Cooper have a metal dick? Talk about fucking like a machine.

Hysterical laughter exploded from him, making it past both of his hands as he slammed them over his mouth.

"God damn it."

Cooper stopped and dropped Alvix to the floor where he convulsed with laughter so hard tears trickled down his cheeks.

"What's going on, LT?" Rivers caught up with them.

Alvix peeked through the strands of hair hanging over his face. They were in a shallow alcove in a hallway, or at least he assumed that's where they were. It wasn't like he had gotten a tour of the place or been allowed to wander around.

"I don't know."

Dark squares of metal ran down both men's left arms to where their hands gripped their guns. *Oh, shit. Patchwork robots.* He fell over, laughing again, stuffing his fist in his mouth to stifle the noise.

"Ummm...LT, we really need to move." Steele peered in at Alvix. "Maybe knock him out or gag him until we're back on the ship."

Helpless to stop, Alvix giggled. Okay, so he wasn't handling things nearly as well as he thought.

"I'm sorry," he gasped. "Maybe you *should* knock me out. I'm not sure I'll be able to control it."

Cooper knelt on one knee next to him and handed his gun to Rivers.

Alvix shrank away when Cooper reached out to touch his shoulder.

"I'll give you a shot of Dicacin. It'll knock you unconscious until we're off planet."

"Please." He nuzzled into Cooper's hand that cupped his cheek.

"No problem. I think you deserve a little rest."

Leaning back against the wall, he watched Rivers draw a syringe full of pale blue liquid. Cooper took the needle and inserted it into Alvix's vein on the inside of his elbow.

"Don't worry. I'll get you out of here," Cooper promised.

Alvix laughed, but this time it sounded harsh. "Good luck with that."

His vision blurred and his head spun.

"Cooper," was all he managed to say before he passed out.

*   *   *

It could have been hours or days before Alvix opened his eyes again. A light purple wall greeted him, and he frowned. The room the Tongassians kept him in was a bland white. Nothing for him to get excited about.

There was something about the wall he stared at now. The purple swirled with white streaks, creating a cloud-like effect. This was familiar.

Rolling onto his back, he kept his eyes open. Somehow, he knew the ceiling would be blue with white streaks. He was in his own room on his own ship. Thank God, he was safe.

Whoosh.

He jerked as the door to his room slid open. Through the low light, Alvix could only see the silhouette of the man standing there. With a pitiful squeak, he scrambled away until his back pressed against the wall and he curled into a ball.

"Hush, Alvix. It's okay. It's me, Cooper. You're safe now. We're off planet."

Alvix squinted in the sudden flood of light. As the tears slowly disappeared and he could see again, he realized it really was Cooper kneeling next to the bed. He gasped and reached out, stopping inches away from the metal now covering all of Cooper's face.

"You can touch." Cooper gave him permission.

Pressing his fingertips to the cool smooth surface, he met Cooper's silver eyes. "What does it feel like?"

Cooper shrugged, though there was no real change in his expression. "A little odd, like I'm wearing a mask. It's flexible and everything. The scientists wanted to ensure we'd still be able to move and fight, no matter how metal we become."

After pushing up onto his knees, Alvix cradled Cooper's face with both hands. He moaned softly. He managed to detect concern in Cooper's gaze.

"You don't have to touch me. I'm sure you'd prefer not being touched by anyone at the moment."

How could he explain that the cold chill of Cooper's new skin soothed him in a deeper way than never being touched again would?

His lips burned as he remembered the ravishing kisses of the Tongassian king. Alvix whimpered and lurched forward, attacking Cooper's mouth with his own. He only wanted to stop the fire that tried to escape from inside him.

Cooper's breath danced over Alvix's lips for a second before their lips met. *Oh, God.* Alvix's brain went blank at the first silken drag of Cooper's metal lips over his own heated human flesh. No words could express how much Alvix wanted to crawl over and smash his entire naked body against Cooper's. Maybe it would douse the heat left under his skin from the fiery attention of his captor.

Icy strips ran down his sides and he realized they were Cooper's hands only when the other man set him away. He whined in protest, wanting more of the satin smooth touch calming his jumpy nerves.

"No, Alvix. You just want me because I rescued you and now you're safe."

He narrowed his eyes and glared at Cooper. "I'm not that mental."

Cooper raised a non-existent eyebrow in skeptical inquiry, and Alvix crossed his arms with an undignified snort.

"All right. Fine. I do have some issues after being some alien torch creature's boy toy. Forgive me if I seem a little clingy to a person who isn't going to flame my insides into a pile of ash while watching me squirm in agony for fun."

Turning to face the wall, he shuddered, pressing one fist to his mouth, suppressing the sobs. His other hand rested on his stomach while he hoped he wouldn't throw up. Great way to convince Cooper he was dealing with the trauma.

The mattress dipped, and he couldn't stop from rolling back into Cooper's personal space. Alvix squished his eyelids together, but tears leaked from the corners anyway. Every atom in his body froze when a cool finger traced the path of one of his tears.

"He did that to you?"

Cooper's soft voice washed over Alvix's ear, bringing more shivers with it. Fuck, he didn't want to go into detail about the torture he'd endured.

"Alvix, answer me."

The determination underlying the command warned Alvix that Cooper wouldn't back down.

Flopping over onto his back, he covered his eyes with one arm while gesturing to his abdomen, where a faint white scar curled from one side of his body to the other just inches above his belly button. Goose bumps rose along his skin as Cooper trailed two fingers along the path of the scar.

"He did this and you lived? How is that even possible?"

Peering out from under his arm, Alvix pinned Cooper with a sardonic expression. "How is it possible you're turning into a living, breathing robot?"

"Science and blind loyalty."

"Hmmm...." He tried to make it sound like a question.

Encouraging Cooper to talk would give Alvix a chance to build his protective walls again. They were slightly charred, but if he could shore them up, Cooper's implied caring wouldn't hurt when the man ditched him. And he would get dumped on the closest inhabited planet. Alvix knew he was too much trouble for Cooper and his men to deal with. It was only obligation and that crazy "leave no one behind" code that brought them back to get him.

"When our superiors informed us about this new specialized unit they wanted to form, my men and I jumped at the chance. Better pay. More chance for faster advancement. Getting an opportunity to check out all the latest weapons first. There couldn't be a downside."

Cooper outlined Alvix's belly button before sliding over the dip where Alvix's hip and torso met. Hiding his eyes, Alvix breathed in, trying to calm his pulse and make sure his cock didn't react to Cooper's touch. An odd indifference in the stroking told Alvix that Cooper wasn't doing any of it on purpose. The other man seemed caught up in memories.

"They gave us physicals and shots, telling us they were super antibiotics created to help us heal from wounds faster. We were the first unit to be given them." Cooper laughed. "Of course, now we know we were the only unit to receive the injections."

Hoping it wouldn't stop Cooper from continuing, Alvix laid a trembling hand on Cooper's back, giving him the only support he could.

"It wasn't until Steele got injured in a fire fight that we began to understand what we'd gotten ourselves into."

Shuffling from across the room brought Cooper out of whatever fugue he'd been in. He shot to his feet, and Alvix mourned the loss of his cool solidness.

"We're getting ready to dock, LT."

"Thanks, Rivers. Inform Callum and Steele. Make sure they're ready to off-load."

"Certainly, sir." Rivers sketched a rather casual salute before leaving.

"Discipline's a little loose, Lieutenant," Alvix quipped, searching for a blanket since he just suddenly realized he was naked.

"We've been together a long time. I'm not big on military protocol." Cooper stalked over to the wall hiding Alvix's closet. After opening the door, he jerked out a shirt and pants.

Alvix caught them as Cooper flung them at him. "Clean up and get dressed. We'll be disembarking soon."

"Where are we?"

"Somewhere safe." Cooper marched toward the door.

"That tells me a whole hell of a lot," Alvix muttered as he watched Cooper practically run screaming from the room.

He climbed off the bed and stood slowly, one hand braced on the wall. Hallelujah, he didn't fall on his face, so it seemed his legs were working again.

Exiting his room five minutes later, he found a stocky man leaning against the wall across the hall from his door.

"LT said I should escort you to the bridge. Figured you might need a hand getting there."

Alvix rolled his eyes. "I was held captive and tortured. That doesn't make me weak or fragile."

"Yeah." The man fell in step beside Alvix. "Does make you a little shaky on your feet, though. Staff Sergeant Steele."

"Are you the token short guy?"

They stopped at an intersection of corridors for Alvix to catch his breath. Steele grinned and winked.

"Sure. But we short guys have our uses. Can sneak into places big guys would get stuck in."

He hadn't thought of that.

"Where are we?"

Steele pursed his lips for a second before shrugging. "Can't see why it'd hurt to tell you."

Hurt who? Did they think he was a spy or something?

"Don't tell me if it's super secret or anything, though I'd like to point out that unless you keep me in complete isolation, I'll see something."

Wonderful. Now he sounded like a snotty teenager pouting because the adults won't tell him anything.

"We're on Tative. Pope's dad owns it."

They halted in front of the elevator, and Steele keyed in some numbers before gesturing for Alvix to precede him into the car.

"Pope?"

"The crispy guy you stopped that Tongassian jerk-off from cooking." Steele pushed the button for the bridge.

"No way. His father owns a planet? What the fuck is the kid doing in the military then?"

He staggered as the elevator jerked into motion. Steele gripped his elbow for a second until he got his balance.

"Family tradition. The kid's father is Supreme General Martin Gateway."

Wow. No wonder he could afford to buy an entire planet.

"How is Pope doing?"

After being subjected himself to the psychotic fun of the Tongassian king, Alvix wondered how the soldier was recovering. Of course, their experiences weren't comparable. No matter how painful it got, Alvix was never in any danger of dying from the fire. Pope wouldn't have survived another encounter.

Steele shrugged. "Haven't seen the kid much. LT keeps us updated, but doctors don't want to risk infection."

"You seem all right."

The car jerked to a stop and Steele shot him a wry smile.

"No worse than other fucked-up situations we'd been in."

"Hey, man, good to see you up and moving around." Callum bounded over to him and slapped his back, almost toppling him onto Steele.

"Jackass. Be careful. Flame here hasn't gotten his legs back completely. You know Dicacin can mess you up for a little bit."

Alvix smiled his thanks to Steele as his escort set him straight. He

31

dropped into a seat, ignoring the faint surge of jealousy at the thought of someone else flying his ship.

"She's a good ship," Rivers complimented him without taking his eyes off the instrument panels in front of him.

"Thanks. She's always been good to me." His hands itched to take up the stick again.

"Where's LT?" Steele dropped into the seat to Alvix's right.

"On the comm with Jensen, making sure everything's ready for us when we land." Callum took the spot next to Rivers, but spun around to face them. "It sounds like we're getting a week's worth of R&R before we head out again."

"Apple won't be ready." Rivers flicked a couple switches.

"Yeah, well, neither will Pope. We'll have to leave them behind. The GalMil isn't going to waste all that money they put into us by letting us get fat and lazy here." Callum winked at Alvix. "Of course, they don't know where 'here' is."

There was something else going on. Some sort of sub-text that Alvix was missing, but he didn't think he wanted to know.

"Hey, dude, I wanted to ask you something, but you've been out like a light since LT shot you full of Dicacin."

Alvix met Callum's curious stare and knew he wasn't going to like the question.

"Maybe you should wait until Flame here has been awake longer. I've been on the receiving end of your questions and it's too easy to get confused."

Steele ran interference for Alvix. It was probably another order from Cooper about not overwhelming the traumatized civilian.

"Ask away, but I reserve the right not to answer."

Callum nodded. "Fair enough."

The younger soldier leaned forward in his chair, his all blue eyes gleaming with curiosity, but before he could ask, a single bell rang, and Rivers shut down Alvix's ship.

"Docking complete. We need to meet LT at the hatch."

Rivers herded them off the bridge and into the elevator like a mother hen corralling her chicks.

"Damn," Callum muttered. "Well, I've still got a week to pin you down and find out what I want to know."

Alvix crossed his arms and tried not to look nervous. Sure, Callum probably wanted to know about the fire-eating thing and that happened to be the one topic he didn't want to talk about.

The elevator fell two decks and slammed to a stop, causing his stomach to hit his feet. Alvix's vision blurred and he paled. "Shit."

When the world stopped spinning, he found himself cradled in Cooper's arms, his cheek resting against a soft piece of fabric.

"Do you have a heartbeat?"

The quirk of concern on Cooper's face became a frown of confusion. "What?"

He patted the well-formed chest under his face. "Do you have a heart beat since you're metal?"

"Yes. My heart hasn't been injured yet."

"Good." He hummed happily. "I like to listen to my lover's heartbeat when I lie in his arms."

Laughter surrounded Alvix and he looked around, suddenly remembering where he was. Callum bent to offer him a hand.

"See, LT, told you he was cute."

The heat his blush generated rivaled the fire he'd roasted in a few days earlier. He scrambled out of Cooper's embrace and stood, trying not to meet anyone's gaze.

"Callum, shut up." Cooper bit the words off, frustration evident in his clenched jaw.

"Yes, sir." Callum snapped a smart salute before ruining it by winking at Alvix again.

Maybe he wasn't winking. Maybe he had a nervous eye tic that made it look like he was winking. Alvix shook his head, exhaustion hitting him hard, even though he had just gotten up. He slumped against a crate, waiting for them to open the hatch. First thing he wanted to know was where his bed was.

The seals hissed open, and four broad backs blocked Alvix's view. Were they that eager to get off the ship?

"Welcome back, Lieutenant Cooper. I'm glad to hear your mission was successful."

When all the shoulders in his line of sight relaxed, a twinge in Alvix's chest pained him. Why were they still trying to keep him safe? He didn't understand the kind of possessive protection they exhibited toward him. He was nothing; just the crazy person who sacrificed himself for them. Guess that earned him some brownie points.

"Supreme General Gateway wishes to make your acquaintance, Captain Alvix."

Peering up, Alvix found everyone else had left except for a slender petite woman. Her red hair pulled back in a ponytail, she looked like she was barely sixteen, but the gun holstered at her hip and the weariness in her eyes told him she was older than her looks said.

Scrubbing his hand through his hair, he grimaced as his fingers caught in tangles. "I know it's bad manners to keep a supreme general waiting, but could I take a long shower and nap before I meet him?"

Her eyebrows shot up and she yelled, "Cooper," as Alvix collapsed.

CHAPTER 5

Scoping Alvix up in his arms, Cooper frowned. "What happened?"

Jensen sniffed her unconcern at his growling attitude. "I told him the general would like to meet him. He asked if he could take a shower and a nap first. Then he fainted."

"Damn. The drug must not be completely out of his system."

Cooper looked down at the man and didn't like how light Alvix felt. He'd been slender before that alien flaming king got a hold of him. Now the man's skin seemed stretched over bone without any fat to fill out the harsh angles.

"I'm afraid General Gateway's going to have to wait, Jensen. There's no way Alvix is going to be functioning at what passes for normal for him."

She thought for a moment before she nodded. "I'll take you to Captain Alvix's room and then go talk to the general. I'm sure he'll understand, considering what his son went through."

"Thank you."

"You're welcome, Lieutenant. The general appreciates all you and your men have done to rescue Corporal Gateway."

Cooper bit his tongue. They might have gone back, but it was because of Alvix that the rest of them were alive. No matter what anyone else said, he wasn't going to forget that.

After arriving at the room, Alvix didn't wake up when Cooper stripped him and tucked him under the blankets, pausing to watch as Alvix embraced a pillow. He patted the man's back before following

Jensen out of the room.

"Will Captain Alvix need a doctor?"

He shrugged. "I didn't see any wounds, but maybe he should be checked out."

"I'll have Doctor Leonoid alerted. When the captain wakes up, the doctor can come and look him over."

"Thank you again." He shut the door behind them. "Does the general want me to report right away or do I have time to clean up and grab something to eat?"

"He's been holding up a briefing until he talked to Captain Alvix, so once I inform him the captain isn't available, he'll probably go into his meeting. You should have time."

"Then I'll wait to hear from you. I'll be in my suite."

They saluted each other, and he wandered down the corridor a few doors away from Alvix's room.

After locking the door behind him, Cooper leaned against it. He rubbed his chin and exhaled sharply. Gods, he was tired. Running to Pope's father had been a brilliant suggestion from Steele. They knew General Gateway wasn't the one who'd set them up. The general had ordered them to Tative, where they dropped off Apple and Pope and re-supplied.

Unfortunately for Alvix, it had taken them over a month to get permission for another rescue mission and even then Pope's father hedged about where they were going.

But they were back and things would be looking up for Alvix, if he managed to re-adjust without too many issues. Cooper snorted. Something told him Alvix already had a ton of baggage before becoming a plaything for an alien. It would simply be how well Alvix dealt with all of it.

Pushing away from the door, he strolled through the room, leaving a trail of clothes behind him. When he was naked and standing in the shower area, he turned the water on and soaked himself in a cascade of warm liquid.

The planet they were on was very primitive. Instead of voice-activated showers, or voice-activated anything for that matter, the people living there used manual devices and ate real food instead of synthetic crap.

He absorbed the warmth and let the shower wash his tension away. He grabbed the soap and grimaced slightly as water hit his metal skin with a soft ting. When the scientists injected him with the nano-mites, he'd asked if water would rust the titanium. They'd reassured him that it was his flesh, just strengthened and mutated.

Great. He was turning into a monster. Hell, all of his men were, except for Pope. The doctors weren't sure why the titanium conversion had stopped after they brought him back to Tative from Tongass. It was like the nano-mites no longer existed in Pope's system.

Cooper turned off the shower, dried off, and stared at his reflection in the large mirror. Once a certain percentage of his body had turned to titanium, the nano-mites didn't wait for an injury before converting the remaining flesh. They invaded and changed anything that wasn't the same as the rest. Slowly, over time, the nano-mites would take over his entire body, turning him and his men into fully functioning metal men. After waking up one morning and discovering half his arm covered in titanium when no injury had occurred, he'd gone to the scientists and confronted them about it.

The scientists assured him that his organs wouldn't suffer the same fate as his skin, unless his entire body suffered such damage that the nano-mites swarmed the dying cells. The nano-mites were creatures created to keep their hosts alive by any means necessary, and Cooper couldn't bring himself to complain out loud about them. He'd volunteered for the project.

Dressing quickly, he pushed those morbid thoughts out of his mind. He glanced longingly at his bed, but his stomach rumbled. Food, visits to Apple and Pope, then a meeting with General Gateway came first before sleep.

"No rest for the wicked," he muttered as he left his room.

"LT, you headed for the dining room?"

He didn't stop, simply let Rivers catch up to him.

"They still have food out? I figured I'd have to raid the kitchen."

"Jensen said Gateway left standing orders that food be ready, no matter what time we got back."

"The general's a good man."

Cooper pushed open the doors to the dining room and found Callum and Steele already there.

None of them saluted him, being too busy eating. He was fine with that. He'd never stood on ceremony with the men in his unit. Each one brought his own know-how and skills to the team, plus their own set of memories. It was the luck-of-the-draw that he ended up with a higher rank than they did.

"How's Flame?" Callum asked between bites of what looked like real steak.

"Flame?" He frowned at the unfamiliar name.

"Yeah, Captain Alvix. Steele started calling him that because, well, it fits." Callum shrugged.

"Ah. He's sleeping. Hasn't been able to shake off the effects of the Dicacin and the shit that Tongassian did to him."

"Speaking of which..."

Steele ignored the warning glance Cooper shot him.

"While Pope, Apple, and I were guests of the king, I saw him do some pretty nasty shit, besides turning Pope crispy. I can't imagine Flame managed to escape all that." Steele looked down at his own hands covered with dark titanium. "How did he survive without ending up scarred?"

"Yeah, and what the hell is a fire-eater anyway?" Callum pushed his empty plate away.

"A fire-eater? You have one here?"

They jumped to their feet, reaching for various weapons as a thin, stooped elderly man scuttled into the room.

Resting his hand on the grip of his gun, Cooper sent the man a narrow-eyed glared. "Who are you?"

"Doctor Leonoid." The doctor wrung his long fingered hands together. "Please, do you really have a fire-eater? Where did you find him? Can I see him?"

"Whoa. Slow down, Doc. We don't know what a fire-eater is, so we can't say if he is one or not. He says he's one and you'll get a chance to look him over when he wakes up."

Cooper waved to his men to relax and sit. Doctor Leonoid didn't pose a threat at the moment, though he was going to have to keep an eye on him to make sure he didn't bother Alvix.

"Oh."

The doctor's disappointment hammered at Cooper, but his main concern would always be Alvix and his men. The transport captain had done something no one else had ever done for Cooper. After giving up his freedom to make sure they survived, Alvix would always have Cooper looking out for him.

"Hey, Doc, how are Apple and Pope doing?" Rivers nodded to a seat at the end of the table.

"Both of the corporals are doing as well as can be expected. Corporal McIntosh's injuries have healed. His mental and emotional wounds are a different story. He chooses not to speak to me."

Cooper frowned at that information. Was there something Apple wasn't telling him? He'd check when he visited the corporal later.

"The damage to Corporal Gateway's body was so severe it will take several months for him to regain any kind of normal strength. Yet..." Doctor Leonoid trailed off, his mind caught in a thought.

"Focus, Doctor." Steele slapped the table, making the silverware and the doctor jump.

"Corporal Gateway's body hasn't been converted yet, though whatever damage done to it has healed for the most part."

Relief welled in Cooper and he bit his lip to keep from grinning. The doctor's statement eased him.

"That's good news," he managed to spit out.

"I guess it is for you." Leonoid shot him an understanding nod. "But I'm not sure if the scientists in charge of your project would be happy. They probably genetically coded the nano-mites to take over every part of your body, except for bone and organs."

Callum grunted and stood. "I'm going to visit Apple for a while."

"I'll be by later tonight," Cooper informed the soldier.

"I'll let him know, LT. Gives him a chance to get ready. He's not big on visitors at the moment."

Callum left, and Cooper studied the food on his plate, delivered by a silent waiter. If he thought too hard on how fucked their mission had been from the start, he'd be hit by a deep depression and fierce rage. None of it was his fault, but he couldn't help accepting responsibility for all of it.

"Eat. Going hungry ain't gonna make it better." Steele pointed at Cooper's plate with his fork.

"Thanks, Mom," he joked.

"My momma believed everything could be cured with food. It was amazing that none of my family weighed a ton." Leonoid grimaced. "We didn't have real food, though. Too poor for that. Had to eat the synthetic stuff."

"And no one gets fat off that shit," Rivers finished the doctor's thought.

They chuckled, and Cooper let go of his guilt enough to eat. Rivers, Steele, and the doctor left before he finished.

The others had been gone for at least ten minutes when the door opened again. Cooper looked up to see Supreme General Martin Gateway standing just inside the threshold.

"Sir." He jumped to his feet and snapped a salute.

39

"At ease, Lieutenant." Gateway shut the door behind him and joined Cooper at the table. "Sit and finish your meal. Your report can wait until you're done."

"Thank you, sir." Cooper sat and tried to finish his meal quickly without making a mess.

The general pinched the bridge of his nose and breathed deeply. If Cooper didn't know better, he would have said the general sighed. Soldiers didn't sigh much. They continued on, marching through battles and injuries. The great ones like Gateway never sighed.

Something in the slump of the general's shoulders drove Cooper to break his private rule about never engaging higher-ranking officers in personal conversations.

"Are you all right, sir?"

Instead of denying any problem, Gateway met his gaze and admitted, "I'm tired, Cooper, and disenfranchised with my fellow generals."

Cooper wasn't sure how to respond to that. Gateway was his commanding officer and Cooper could get in trouble for anything he said. He opened his mouth to make a sound, hoping Gateway saw it as encouragement.

Holding up a hand, the general stopped him. "In this room, I'm not Supreme General Gateway, Cooper. I'm a fellow soldier and a father whose son has returned to him broken in every possible way."

"Would you like a drink?" Cooper caught the attention of one of the servers, who brought over a decanter of liquor and two faceted glasses. At the general's nod, Cooper poured them each a finger of it.

Gateway picked his up, toasted Cooper with it and drank it down before Cooper had a chance to sip his own drink.

"When Alexander told me he was going into the military, my pride was thrilled. My only son, the center of my world, was following in my footsteps." He splashed more liquor into his glass and gulped it down in one long swallow.

Cooper kept his mouth shut. He didn't have children and never would, so his understanding was limited.

"After boot camp, he explained that he volunteered for your unit because you were the best and he wanted to learn from you." The general snorted. "Being the proud parent I was, I ensured Alexander was placed with you."

"Little did you know what your son was getting into." Cooper swirled the amber liquid around his glass.

Gateway nodded and shoved his empty glass away. "If I had any idea what was going on with you, I never would've let him join. I'd have made him become an accountant or an insurance salesman."

Cooper's face twisted into a grimace of a smile. "Instead of a monster out of someone's disturbed nightmares."

"Yes." He sent Cooper an apologetic grin. "Sorry."

Shrugging, Cooper stood. "Not your fault if it's true. None of us would have chosen this if we knew how it was going to end."

"And if the whole robot man-of-steel thing wasn't bad enough, I have to worry about my enemies trying to harm me through my son." The general rested his elbows on the table and buried his face in his hands.

"That's the easiest of our problems to solve, General. It might take a little longer, but we'll figure out who ordered our trip to Tongass and who paid to have Pope captured." Cooper stopped pacing and held out his hands, now entirely covered by black flexible titanium. "How this experiment ends is what frightens me, but to be honest, I think your son is reverting back to his natural flesh. Maybe the fire destroyed the nano-mites."

A knock sounded on the door and General Gateway barked out an entrance order. Jensen pushed open the door and saluted.

"Yes, Jensen?"

"Sorry to interrupt, sir, but you asked to be notified when Captain Alvix was awake."

"Thank you."

The general stood and motioned for Cooper to accompany him. "The young captain will be nervous around me, which is understandable. Not many transport pilots want a face-to-face meeting with one of the supreme generals."

"Most GalMil soldiers would prefer to go their whole careers without meeting one," Cooper muttered as he trailed behind Gateway and Jensen.

"True. Captain Alvix will be more at ease with someone he knows there."

"You're not going to interrogate him, are you, sir?"

Gateway shook his head. "No. I'm simply going to give him his heart's desire."

Imagining what Alvix's heart's desire might be was difficult for Cooper. The transport pilot seemed like a normal guy, except for the fire-eating thing. It was that ability which might explain Weldon's desire to get a hold of Alvix.

Who knew what secret wishes lurked in Alvix's soul? Cooper hoped the man took advantage of the general's generosity.

CHAPTER 6

Pressing as tight as he could to the window, Alvix absorbed the chill from the glass. His clothes buffered him from some of the cold, but proper etiquette frowned upon greeting a supreme general in the nude.

He rested his forehead on the pane in front of him and stared at his reflection. God, he was skin and bones. Whatever fat he'd had before had been burnt from him. The plus side was he could feel the cold better and until he could get the internal fire back under control, he'd take being cold as a bonus.

Someone knocked and he turned.

"Come in," he called.

Cooper looked around the edge of the door. He saw the quick full body glance Cooper gave him.

"Don't worry. I'm dressed."

"May the general join us?"

"It's his planet." Alvix waved them in.

The soldier and an older man entered. Alvix strolled over to where two chairs sat at angles to a fireplace.

"Captain Alvix, this is Supreme General Gateway. Supreme General, this is the man who allowed your son to come home to you." Cooper introduced them.

"Sir." He offered his hand, uncomfortable with what Cooper had said.

"Captain, you don't know what you did for me. Alexander is my only son and my entire world." General Gateway shook Alvix's hand and slapped him on a shoulder.

"It wasn't anything special, sir. I'm sure any of the men in your son's unit would've done the same."

"Well, yes, they would have, but I fear they might not have been as successful as you were." Gateway gestured to the chairs. "Please, may we sit? I was up late last night with Alexander."

"Certainly."

Alvix sat, and the general took the other chair. Cooper stood on the hearth, hands clasped behind his back.

"If Alexander is your whole world, why did you let him enter the military?" Alvix frowned. "Even I, who don't pay all that much attention to what goes on around me, have heard of you. You should have stopped him."

He glanced up when Cooper coughed, and saw shock on the man's face.

"What?"

"Alvix, you don't talk to a supreme general like that." Cooper shook his head.

"No, Lieutenant. Captain Alvix is right. I knew the dangers of a career in the military, but the idea of my name living on in the annals of history blinded me. Alexander's eagerness to please me drove him to make some choices he might not have made otherwise."

Guilt shone in the general's eyes, and Alvix decided Gateway might not be such a bad guy if he could admit to being wrong.

"Yeah, well, it's too late to second guess yourself now." He dug his fingers into his twitching thigh muscles. God, he hoped neither man noticed his tremors.

"Has Doctor Leonoid been in to see you?"

"Not yet. I told the guard outside my door I wanted to see you and get some food. A doctor can't help me. Time's really the only thing that can cure what's wrong with me."

He shuddered at the thought of being poked and prodded by some doctor, especially if said doctor knew about his fire-eating.

"I'm surprised. He seemed rather interested in this fire-eating power of yours." Cooper eyed him.

"It's nothing special. I just need to eat and rest for a couple of days, then I'll be good as new."

The general didn't look any more convinced than Cooper did.

"Would you humor me and allow the doctor to examine you? It

would make me feel better if he can reassure me there's no permanent damage."

If a person was smart, he didn't say no to an order presented as a request. Alvix never claimed to be a genius, but he knew he didn't have a choice.

"Of course, sir, but I'd like Cooper to be present when the doctor's here."

General Gateway's curiosity almost got the best of his manners. Alvix could tell, by the way the older man started to say something and then stopped.

"Also understand this. No matter what the doctor tells you, I won't be a guinea pig. Just because I'm a freak doesn't mean people can treat me as a specimen."

The general blinked at the vehement tone of Alvix's voice.

"You have my word. You'll be free to go when you feel ready. I won't hold you against your will."

Right. The man sounded sincere, but Alvix wasn't willing to trust him any farther than he could throw the man. The GalMil believed they were above common courtesy and rules. A supreme general, within said organization, could come to the conclusion his word was law, even to a civilian.

"I have one last question." Gateway paused.

"Go ahead. Ask, but you asking doesn't mean I'm answering." Alvix settled into the chair.

"Fair enough. What do you want as a reward for saving my son?"

"I didn't do it for your son." He shrugged, but managed not to look at Cooper.

"Hmmm..."

"Give me a hundred credits and drop me at the nearest spaceport. I don't need anything special."

General Gateway nodded. "I'll work on that."

"General, your next briefing starts in ten minutes." Jensen's voice interrupted the silence.

"I'm on my way," Gateway replied into a receiver on his wrist. "Inform Doctor Leonoid that Captain Alvix will consent to an examination."

"Of course, sir. He's on his way."

The general stood and held out his hand to Alvix. "Thank you, again, for saving my son's life. I'm hoping we'll be able to talk more before I have to leave."

Alvix shook the man's hand and nodded, unsure what else they had to say to each other. He never imagined he'd meet a general, especially under these circumstances.

Cooper saluted Gateway, and they watched the general leave. After a few minutes of quiet, Alvix snorted.

"Weirdest moment of my life."

He jerked to his feet. The flat, hard surface of the window called to him. His body remembered how cool it felt. Without any real thought, he strolled to it, curled up on the seat in front of the window and laid his cheek on the smooth glass.

"You okay?" Cooper stood a few feet away, concern evident in his voice, if not his face.

"Yes." He exhaled softly. "It's hot in here."

It was a crazy statement because Alvix knew the room probably was a comfortable temperature for Cooper and anyone else, but his body burned hotter than normal and even more so after transmuting all the fire he'd bathed in over the last month or so.

"Is it always like this for you?" Cooper edged closer.

He rubbed harder against the glass. "Yes. I'm usually the hottest one in the room and I don't mean looks-wise."

Cooper chuckled like Alvix wanted, and he watched the other man relax even more. He motioned a hand at one of the chairs.

"You can sit. The doctor should be here soon, now he knows I'm awake."

"Considering how his ears perked up when I mentioned fire-eating, I'm surprised he's not out in the hallway, pacing."

When Cooper sat, he chose to share the seat Alvix was on instead of his own chair. Alvix stretched out and let his bare foot touch Cooper's thigh.

The jolt of electricity raced from the sole of his foot to his groin. He shifted, trying not to make his condition obvious. Maybe it was a good thing he wasn't naked since there wouldn't be any way to hide his erection and the effect Cooper had on him.

He closed his eyes as Cooper wrapped his hand around his ankle and stroked along his skin. Swallowing a groan, he longed to ask Cooper to run his hand all over his body. Considering the fact the lieutenant thought Alvix was damaged goods, there was no way Cooper would continue touching him further, even if he asked.

"Have others tried experimenting on you?" Cooper's question barely reached Alvix's ears.

"Not me. I seem to fall in the torturing and toying with category. I've seen others of my kind disappear behind the walls of labs, never to be seen again."

"How many of your 'kind' are there?"

Was this the gentler, kinder form of interrogation? Did Cooper really want to know or was he fact-gathering for the general?

Alvix rocked his forehead on the window. "I'm not sure. I used to live with a group of six or seven. By the time I was sixteen, the others had vanished. Some went to the labs. Some died because life on the street can be dangerous. Others, I don't know where they went."

He grimaced as the memory of the last time he saw another fire-eater popped up in his mind. "The last one I saw gave me to Weldon to pay off his drug debt. That's why I disappeared, and why you would never have been able to find me."

The hand around his ankle tightened. What part of his story was upsetting Cooper?

"Took me two years of torture at Weldon's hands to figure out I was never going to pay off that debt. Weldon wasn't about to let such a valuable piece of property go."

"So you ran away," Cooper murmured, his fingers caressing again.

"Yeah, stowed away on a transport ship. Somehow, luck was with me. They were down a crewmember when the captain discovered I was on board. I ended up working for him for five years. Took my pilot's test two years ago and got my ship last year."

"You've done well for yourself."

"It's a living. I'm never going to be rich, but at least I can eat." He shrugged.

A rather excited knock echoed around the room. Muscles tensing, Alvix didn't want to grant the doctor permission to enter.

"Get it over with and then you can eat."

Nausea roiled in Alvix's stomach. At that moment, food didn't sound good.

Cooper stood and went to open the door. A small, pointy-faced man stepped in, his inquisitive eyes searching the room until his gaze landed on Alvix.

"Oh, my God, you *are* real."

CHAPTER 7

Alvix froze as Leonoid rushed at him. Shit, the doctor was going to touch Alvix, and Cooper had the oddest feeling that wouldn't be a good thing. He moved quickly to block the doctor.

"Doctor Leonoid, I'd like you to meet Captain Alvix."

Leonoid pulled up, barely keeping from hitting Cooper in the chest.

"Right. It's nice to meet you, Captain. General Gateway ordered me to exam you and make sure you're not suffering any wounds from your ordeal." Leonoid eyed Cooper. "If you could give us some privacy, Lieutenant."

"I'm not—" he started.

"He's not..." Alvix interrupted.

"Leaving." They finished together.

"Well, the best place to examine you would be at my lab. I'd be happy to escort you there."

Alvix shook his head so hard Cooper feared the man would fall off the window seat. "You'll check me over here, Doctor. I don't need to be poked or prodded. I'm doing this to make the general happy. There's nothing wrong with me that rest and food can't heal."

"We'll see." Leonoid's jaw looked like the doctor was clenching his teeth. "Cooper, turn the lights up as bright as they go. Captain, strip and stand over here."

As he went to the light panel, Cooper tried to ignore the rustle of clothing behind him. The kiss he'd shared earlier with Alvix still played on his mind. He'd pushed Alvix away and managed some lame excuse about the man being grateful to him for the rescue. Now, Cooper had been on the receiving end of several grateful kisses, none of which had felt like Alvix's. He might be thankful Cooper came back for him, but there had been a lot of need in that kiss as well.

"You have quite a few scars, Captain Alvix, but none of them look recent."

Cooper turned and saw Leonoid tracing each white line on Alvix's skin. Alvix winced or grimaced at each touch. What didn't Alvix like about the doctor? The pilot never seemed upset when Cooper touched him.

"I heal fast."

Alvix caught Cooper's gaze and rolled his eyes. Cooper understood Alvix wasn't going to offer up any extra information than necessary to the doctor.

Tuning out Leonoid's mumblings, Cooper studied the naked man in front of him. Every inch of Alvix's lean, light gold body flipped all of Cooper's switches, even some he didn't know he had. When he got to the thick, but average length cock nestled in a bed of black curls at Alvix's groin, Cooper's mouth watered, eager to feel it on his tongue. That thought shocked him since he'd never had the urge to suck any man's prick before.

He'd never gotten excited about blowing a guy. Oh, he loved fucking and getting fucked, plus if his bed partner offered him a blow job, he never turned him down. He just never offered to return the favor.

Yet here Cooper stood, fighting the need to drop to his knees, wrap his hand around Alvix's shaft, and take the man in until he buried his nose in those curls. Smothering a moan, Cooper started to turn away. Something in Leonoid's hand caught his attention. He struck before his mind registered what it was.

"You little shit." He knocked the lighter from the doctor's hand. It skittered to a stop by the door.

Alvix glanced over his shoulder at Leonoid. "You couldn't resist."

"Lieutenant Cooper, do you know what he is? I've heard of fire-eaters, but never seen one. We could learn so much about him if I could just study him."

"He is in the room, Leonoid, and General Gateway has already given the captain his word that no testing or studying will take place. If you get out of here and leave Alvix alone, I might forget about what you just did."

Twisted longing showed in Leonoid's eyes as the doctor exited the room. Cooper waited until the door shut before approaching Alvix and checking the burn site. There wasn't a blister or anything, just a small red spot. He lightly ran the pad of his finger over it.

"Thank you." Alvix brushed his hand over Cooper's chest as he inched away to curl up on the seat by the window again. He was still naked.

"You're welcome."

He wanted to snatch up the pile of discarded clothes, throw them at Alvix, and order the man to get dressed. Just because he was uncomfortable with it, though, didn't give him the right to demand anything of Alvix.

"Why the window? Do you like to flaunt your assets to everyone wandering around outside?"

Alvix gazed at the glass as Cooper paced. What was out there that so fascinated the man? Cooper was about to ask again when he realized that Alvix's eyes followed him as he moved around the room.

Their gazes locked, and Cooper strolled over, sitting next to Alvix's hip. His thigh brushed the curve of Alvix's ass, and Alvix's breath caught.

"Why the window?" He took a chance and caressed the nape of Alvix's neck.

"It's cool and soothes the heat in me."

Alvix's eyes drifted shut, freeing Cooper to do more than look. Leaning forward, he rubbed his lips over Alvix's shoulder. A shuddering sigh wracked the naked body.

Easing back, he said, "I'll get the kitchen to bring you some food."

Alvix nodded, but didn't move. Cooper went to the intercom by the bed and requested food be sent to Alvix's room. When he finished, he returned, lifted Alvix, and settled the slender man on his lap.

He encircled Alvix's waist, but didn't tighten his grip because of the slight quiver of tension in Alvix's body.

"Is this all right?"

He should have asked permission before manhandling Alvix. After everything that had happened, getting poked in the ass by Cooper's erection could bring back bad memories.

Silence met his questions. Was Alvix going to answer? He got ready to set Alvix away from him. At that moment, Alvix relaxed against him, laid his head on Cooper's shoulder and slid his arm around Cooper's waist.

He nuzzled his face into Alvix's curls and released all the tension in his own body. There would be time to worry about all the troubles lining up outside Alvix's door. He'd need to talk to the guys and General Gateway about their next mission. In addition to searching for the bastard who set them up, something needed to be done with Pope and Apple.

Cooper's thoughts stuttered to a halt as Alvix dragged his lips over his chest. *Shit.* The heat rolling off Alvix was unbelievable.

"God, you're hot."

When Alvix's shoulders twitched, Cooper worried he might have insulted the man, until a soft laugh reached his ears. He thought about what he said. Chuckling, he ran his fingers down Alvix's sides, drawing more laughter.

"You know what I meant."

Alvix gasped and nodded. Bracing his body as far away from Cooper as he could, Alvix grinned. "I know. My internal temperature is higher at the moment because of all the fire I've absorbed over the past month."

"Mmm..." Cooper grunted, not sure if he wanted to continue that line of conversation.

When he didn't ask any follow-up questions, Alvix nestled close to him again. Cooper noticed Alvix touched the window with the palm of his hand.

The easy silence broke with a knock on the door. Cooper set Alvix to the side, tossing him a blanket before answering the summons. A private stood in the hallway with a tray cart. Cooper shoved the door wider, allowing the man to enter. The private set up the food for Alvix.

"I'm going to see Apple and Pope. Would you mind if I stopped by to see you afterward?" he asked after the private left.

Alvix shrugged as he reached for one of the sandwiches. "If you want. How are your friends doing?"

"Apple's doing all right physically, but mentally he's not always there." He scrubbed his hand over his jaw. "Pope's getting better. He still has days when he's in pain or has nightmares."

"It'll take a long time for the memories to dull. I wish I could say they'll disappear, but that will never happen." Alvix stared down at the table, fidgeting with the silverware. "Why do you call Alexander 'Pope'?"

"We call him Pope because he likes poetry and shit like that. He used to talk about all the old Earth poets and one was Alexander Pope, so Rivers started calling him Pope."

"Poetry? Maybe one of you should read some of it to him. Might help with the nightmares."

"That's a good idea. I'll see if Steele can do it." He edged over to where Alvix sat and leaned down to kiss him on the forehead. "I'll stop by to check on you."

Alvix's stunned expression struck Cooper and he laughed. Guess Alvix wasn't expecting that.

He whistled as he left, not completely understanding why, but his heart was light for the first time in several months.

CHAPTER 8

Stomach full and alone again, Alvix draped the blanket over his shoulders before returning to the window. It wasn't the coolness he sought this time. Night had fallen and stars seemed suspended in a velvet sky. All the planets he'd visited over the years of transporting, he'd never been to one so pristine. There didn't seem to be many people or cities around.

No lights polluted his vision and the darkness revealed the reason why he loved traveling through space. Solitude and infinity. People had been exploring the universe for centuries yet no one had found the end of it.

He spied Cooper slipping into the room behind him. "Have you ever sat outside and stared up at the stars?"

"I wasn't sure you were still up. Why are you sitting in the dark?" Cooper joined him at the window.

He shrugged. "My eyes hurt from the light and I like the dark."

"Makes sense." Cooper laid his hand on Alvix's shoulder. "Would you like to go outside into the garden?"

Shooting a quick glance at Cooper, Alvix nodded. "I'd like that, if it's allowed."

"Allowed? Why wouldn't it be? Though you should get dressed."

He took the hand Cooper held out to him and let the man pull him to his feet. "I figured the general wouldn't want me wandering around the place." Alvix jerked open the closet door, not sure if he'd find anything in there.

A few shirts and pants hung there. He picked one of each, quickly dressing.

"The general isn't worried about you. As far as he's concerned, you're an honored guest because of saving Pope."

"Whatever." He sat and slipped into his boots. "Let's go."

Cooper grabbed a couple of blankets before leading the way out of the room. Alvix kept his gaze moving, even though he wouldn't have been able to describe the house afterward. He simply didn't want to be caught staring at Cooper's ass.

"Where is this place? Didn't you say the general owned this planet?"

"If anyone can own a planet. Actually, one of the general's ancestors discovered Tative while trolling around the universe. He didn't tell anyone except his son. Its location has been passed down from father to son."

"Hell of an inheritance." He chuckled. "The only thing my ancestors gave me was the ability to survive being burnt to a crisp."

"My parents dumped me at the military academy when I was five. That was the last time I saw them." Cooper held open a door for Alvix to go through.

Alvix never figured out what made him stop right in front of Cooper and meet the man's gaze. Going up on the tips of his toes, he kissed Cooper. One quick peck and he moved on.

One step and he stood outside under a dark sky littered with bright pinpoints of light. His lungs filled with pure clean air and his natural internal fire cooled slightly.

"Follow me. I know a place we can spread one of the blankets. It's far enough from the house, the lights won't mess up the view."

"I'd follow your ass anywhere," Alvix muttered as he trailed after Cooper.

Cooper hesitated for a second. Did he hear what Alvix said? Alvix shrugged and decided not to worry about it. It wasn't as if Cooper didn't know Alvix was interested in him. It was up to the soldier to make the next move.

"Were you able to see your friends?"

"Yes. Apple still isn't talking, but at least his wounds have healed. Pope's talking, yet his body is raw and painful for the most part. He'd like to see you if you're up to visiting him." Cooper hunched his shoulders. "He isn't very nice to look at, though."

He caught up to Cooper and laid his hand on the man's lower back.

"I've seen people with burns all over their bodies. Your friend won't bother me. I'd be happy to go and talk to him."

Nodding, Cooper pointed to a clearing that seemed to be at the exact center of the garden. They spread out one of the blankets, and Alvix flopped down on his back, sighing and staring at the sky. Cooper joined him and covered both of them with the other blanket.

Surprise hit him when Cooper reached out and snagged him, tucking him tight to Cooper's side. He flung his arm over Cooper's stomach and savored the coolness seeping into his body from the man's titanium skin.

The silence falling over them wasn't oppressive or uncomfortable. It lulled Alvix into a light doze. The steady beat of Cooper's heart thrummed through Alvix's body and settled in his groin, making it throb in a matching rhythm.

He slipped his hand under the hem of Cooper's T-shirt, stroking along the waistband of the man's pants. Cooper's muscles twitched, but he didn't stop Alvix from touching him. He plucked at the buttons keeping Cooper under wraps. The halt he was expecting came when Cooper covered his hand with his own large one.

"You don't have to do anything," Cooper reassured him.

Pushing up on one elbow, Alvix looked down into Cooper's silver eyes and nodded. "I know, but I want to."

Cooper cradled his face with his free hand. "Are you sure? I know what the Tongassian did to you. I don't want you to have any flashbacks or anything like that. I'd like this to be a good memory for you."

Alvix nuzzled into Cooper's palm for a moment before smiling. "Nothing about you will remind me of him. His touch burned me. Your skin soothes me. He made me scream with pain. I'll scream with pleasure because of you."

Whatever Cooper saw in Alvix's face must have convinced him that Alvix meant every word he said. He stretched his hands over his head and grinned up at Alvix. "Then I'm all yours."

For tonight at least, Alvix's inner voice reminded him and he mentally shrugged. He wasn't looking for anything more than a moment in time. Forever didn't exist in his vocabulary or his life. People had always walked away from him and never looked back.

But Cooper came back for you. That was true as far as it went. Cooper returned for him out of obligation and that silly ingrained honor code. While Alvix appreciated the rescue, he wasn't stupid enough to think it meant anything more than payment for a debt owed.

He gave himself a shake. The night was waning and he couldn't chance Cooper changing his mind when the sun rose.

His fingers fumbled at the buttons at Cooper's groin. As much as he wanted to touch all of Cooper's dark, smooth body, he wanted to feel the man's prick in his mouth. It was a burning desire to drink Cooper's seed, tasting the familiar salty bitterness of cum flavored with Cooper's own special essence.

Cooper shivered as the cool night air hit his hard cock when Alvix revealed it to the darkness. Alvix hummed and ran his finger down the length of it.

"Very pretty," he murmured.

A choked laugh came from Cooper. "Will you think it's pretty when it's like the rest of me?"

"Well, considering I get hard the moment I see you, I don't think you have anything to worry about in that department." He fisted Cooper's shaft and pumped.

"Ah." Cooper arched off the ground.

Alvix pushed the top blanket off them and slid down to sprawl between Cooper's spread thighs. He licked the spongy head of Cooper's cock, letting the man's pre-cum coat his tongue. He kept stroking with one hand, while fondling Cooper's heavy balls in the other hand. His own erection pressed against the stiff fabric of his pants, informing Alvix it wouldn't be long after Cooper came that Alvix would spill his seed as well.

Saliva pooled in his mouth as he swallowed Cooper down, taking as much of his cock as he could until the head hit the back of his throat. For the first time, his non-existent gag reflex made him happy.

"Fuck."

He glanced up to see Cooper braced on his hands looking down at him. He winked, and Cooper groaned, his fingers flexing into the ground underneath them. Cooper's legs shifted restlessly and he shoved a little deeper into Alvix's mouth.

Alvix took the hint. He started moving, bobbing his head up and down as he synchronized his hand to the same rhythm. His spit eased the friction between their flesh. Cooper's balls tightened and drew closer to his body. Alvix squeezed them, tugging just a little before tickling the skin right behind them.

Cooper collapsed on his back, shuddering as Alvix scraped his teeth down the sides of the turgid shaft in his mouth. He pressed the flat of his tongue to the pulsing vein along the underside of Cooper's cock. More pre-cum leaked from Cooper, and Alvix drank it up, looking forward to the cum he'd be feasting on in a few seconds.

"Alvix," Cooper warned, but Alvix wasn't going to pull away.

He popped off for a moment, stabbed the point of his tongue into Cooper's slit and the man shouted. Without giving him time to think, Alvix went all the way down on his prick again, working the heated flesh with his throat muscles.

"Shit."

He smiled inside as Cooper exploded in his mouth, flooding his throat with ropey strings of cum. He drank it like it was the sweetest space wine, licking and sucking until Cooper softened. Easing away, he let Cooper slide out of his mouth and he placed a gentle kiss on the crown of Cooper's cock.

"Come here." Cooper waved a flopping hand at him.

Crawling up Cooper's body, Alvix tried to ignore the ache in his dick until he could thrust against Cooper's thigh. He moaned and sucked in his stomach, letting Cooper get his pants open and fish out his cock.

"Cooper."

His eyes rolled in his head as Cooper's cold hand encircled his shaft. Most men would shy away from Cooper's metallic touch, but Alvix found the touch intoxicating. He plunged through the tight tunnel Cooper created with his fingers. Panting, Alvix buried his face in the crook of Cooper's neck.

The tingling at the base of his spine rocketed through his body along the nerves. Hot liquid blanketed his cock, Cooper's hand, and stomach. Cooper didn't let go until Alvix slumped to the side and heaved a shuddering breath.

"Are you okay?"

Alvix glanced over at Cooper, hearing the concern in the man's question. He nodded as he grabbed the corner of the blanket and wiped all their sticky parts clean.

"I'm fine, Cooper. No horrible flashbacks or weird moments. There's nothing in what we did that reminded me of what I went through." He patted Cooper's stomach and fastened the man's pants.

Cooper lay still, not interfering as Alvix tucked himself away before snuggling close again. Cooper settled his arm around Alvix's waist, embracing him without smothering him.

"Thank you," he said softly, his eyes closed as he drifted on the waves of satisfaction rippling through him.

"You're welcome." Cooper grunted and wiggled. "We should go inside before you catch a cold or something."

"That won't happen. You could drop me off on the coldest planet you know and I'd survive. Besides, I like being outside."

"Then we'll stay outside."

He tugged the blanket over them and squirmed, finding the right spot on Cooper's chest to lay his head. He fell asleep to the slow beat of Cooper's heart, thinking as he did so how perfect this one moment had been.

CHAPTER 9

Cooper glanced up from his breakfast plate when the dining room door opened. Alvix peered in, his face lighting up for an instant at the sight of Cooper. He smiled and waved the man in.

"Join us. The server will bring you a plate. You want java or juice?"

Alvix sat next to him, brushing his ankle with his foot. "Juice, please."

Steele, Rivers, and Callum nodded their good mornings while they finished eating. Cooper was already done, but he poured another cup of java and leaned back in his chair.

"What's the plan for today, LT?" Rivers didn't look up from the instructional manual he was studying.

"I'm meeting with General Gateway to find out what our new orders will be. I want you all to practice weapons and hand-to-hand combat training. Take Apple with you. He's healthy enough to train again. Maybe it'll help snap him out of his funk."

"Not sure if that's the way to do it," Callum commented. The private fiddled with his spoon. "Might push him further into his shell."

"We have to do something, Callum. The doctor says he's fine except for his mental problems. I don't want him to lose his edge because we're treating him like a china doll." Cooper's cup thudded on the table when he set it down.

Alvix stayed quiet, though Cooper welcomed the light caress of Alvix's hand on his thigh. He'd carried Alvix back inside just before dawn. After tucking the man into his bed, Cooper had returned to his own room to get ready to face the day. By the happy look on the man's face, waking up alone didn't bother Alvix.

"We can't know for sure that the GalMil won't send Apple out on a mission with us. He's the best demo man the military has, and they aren't known for being sympathetic to post-battle stress." Steele slathered jelly on a piece of toast. "The only one we're definitely leaving behind is Pope."

Alvix shifted in his chair and cleared his throat. Cooper saw his eyes widened when everyone looked at him.

"You know how damn creepy your eyes are?" He trembled a little, causing Cooper to reach out and squeeze his hand.

"Yeah. It took all of us a while to get used to them. I still get startled when I look in a mirror." Rivers blinked his eyes.

"None of you have pupils. Is that another one of their advance weapon systems or something?"

They weren't really supposed to talk about the experiments, but Cooper had already told Alvix more than Alvix's security clearance said he should know.

"Yes. They give us infrared and night vision. Useful on missions. Not very practical for everyday living." Cooper lifted the corner of his mouth in a rueful smile.

"I guess it fits in well with the whole package." Alvix picked a muffin from his plate and tore it in half. "I could go talk to Pope while you're doing your thing."

"Why?" Callum held up his hands when Cooper glared at him. "Hey, I'm only asking why he'd want to do that. It's not like we were all best friends before our last mission, and it was because of us he was held captive by an asshole."

Alvix patted Cooper's hand when he would have growled at Callum for his callous words. "It's all right. Being held captive by a few assholes doesn't faze me anymore. The thing is, I know what Pope went through. I've felt fire burn my flesh to ashes. My brain has almost boiled in my skull."

Grimacing, Rivers pushed his eggs away.

"You all go and talk to him, but you don't truly understand what he's been through. None of you have burned like he has." Alvix shrugged. "I have, plus I'm not a team member. He doesn't have to act macho around me. I won't think any less of him if he cries or screams."

"We wouldn't either," Cooper protested.

"Of course not, but Pope looks up to all of you. God, he probably worships the very ground you all walk on. He doesn't want to lose any respect he might have with you by acting less than a man."

The room was quiet as the men considered what Alvix had said. Cooper nodded. The man was right. Pope seemed to have them all on pedestals and the kid wanted his own. Maybe the only way he thought he could get one was by acting like his ordeal didn't affect him, even though they all knew it had.

"He's right, LT." Steele regarded Alvix with a stern gaze. "You talk with Pope, but don't force the kid to tell you anything he don't want to. No point in re-hashing shit the mind docs questioned him about."

"We'll talk about what he wants to talk about. I've got nothing but time at the moment, and nowhere I need to be."

"Good." Cooper stood. "Everyone finished?"

His men shoved their last bites into their mouths and nodded. Alvix hadn't eaten more than a few bites, but he stood as well. When Cooper eyed his plate, Alvix pressed a hand to his stomach.

"Not very hungry in the morning."

Cooper let it go. He'd be around for lunch and make sure Alvix ate more then.

"I'll take Alvix to Pope before I meet with the general. You gather up Apple and get to training. We'll all meet back up for lunch at thirteen-hundred hours."

"Yes, sir."

All three men saluted him, and Alvix sketched a little hand wave. Shaking his head, Cooper clasped Alvix's elbow and led the man out of the dining room. When they got out into the hallway, he slid his hand down to grasp Alvix's. The other man glanced down at their entwined fingers, but didn't say anything.

"Did you sleep well?"

Alvix nodded. "Best rest I've had in a long time."

"Good. I had an early morning meeting with our quartermaster. That's why I wasn't there when you woke up."

"You didn't have to explain, but thank you."

His cheeks heated and he wondered if Alvix could tell he was blushing. "I just didn't want you to think I didn't want to share a bed with you."

Alvix pulled him to a stop and glanced around to make sure they were alone. After determining there wasn't anyone else in the corridor with them, Alvix slid his hand behind Cooper's head and drew his mouth down to his. Their first good morning kiss was gentle and held the promise of being more later on. Cooper only let it last for a minute before he reluctantly inched away. He couldn't go to his meeting with the general sporting a boner.

"We aren't married or even in a committed relationship, Cooper. At the moment, we're just friends who got off with each other last night." Alvix pursed his kiss-swollen lips. "I'm not saying there couldn't be more than that between us, but for right now, it is what it is, and let's enjoy it."

He thought about it for a few minutes and decided Alvix was right. Cooper had too many other problems to deal with and starting any kind of serious relationship would take more energy than he had at the moment.

"Maybe once I figure out who betrayed us."

Alvix placed a finger over his lips, not letting him finish. "Don't say it. I don't need pretty promises and sweet words. We'll ride this ship wherever it leads us and have fun until it stops. Now, take me to Pope."

Cooper kissed Alvix's finger and nodded. "He's in the west wing of the house. It's close to his father's suite, so the general can visit him whenever he has a free moment."

"The doctor won't be around, will he?"

"I'm not sure if he will or not. If he bothers you, just have one of the guards stationed outside Pope's room come and get me."

"You're going to rescue me again?" Alvix bumped their shoulders together.

"Well, isn't that what men of steel are good at? Rescuing people?"

Alvix lifted his hands. "I don't know. You and your friends are the only steel men I know."

"Yeah, we're a rare breed, that's for sure."

He paused in front of a set of large wooden doors. Two guards stood watch on each side. They saluted him before allowing him and Alvix through.

"Security's tighter in this wing." Alvix studied the soldiers standing at parade rest at intervals down the hallway.

"The general isn't taking any chances with Pope. We have no way of knowing whether their enemies know about Tative. If they do, they could send an assassin for either the general or Pope." Cooper acknowledged each salute as they walked toward the last two sets of doors.

"Smart thinking." Alvix eyed him. "Do you think they'll try

something here in the general's own house?"

"I have no idea, but it pays to be paranoid and expect the worse."

One of the armed guards at the second to last door opened it, and Cooper nodded to him. As they slipped in, he spotted Leonoid standing next to Pope's bed, a knife in his hand and an unconscious Pope's wrist slit open.

Before he could say anything, Alvix shot past him and slammed into Leonoid, forcing the doctor to drop the knife. He caught Leonoid as Alvix slung him back toward the door. Cooper shook the skinny man.

"Lieutenant Cooper," Leonoid stuttered as fear blossomed in his rheumy blue eyes.

"What the fuck were you doing to Pope?" He snarled, fighting the strong need to rip the doctor apart.

"Just running a test on him."

"What the hell kind of test needs you to slit his wrist open?" He shook the man again as he yelled, "Corporal."

"Sir?"

"Confine the doctor to his quarters and inform Supreme General Gateway that I need to speak to him in his son's room."

"Yes, sir." The guard marched Leonoid off while the doctor protested his treatment.

Turning back to the bed, he found Alvix sitting next to Pope, his hand wrapped around the kid's wrist. He blinked, not sure if he was actually seeing what looked like blue flame sparking between Alvix's fingers. Pope shifted, but didn't regain consciousness, and Alvix hushed him.

"Is he okay?" Cooper approached the bed cautiously, not wanting to surprise either man.

Nodding, Alvix removed his hand from Pope's arm. Cooper's eyebrows shot up when he saw a solid white scar running along the cut Leonoid had made.

"Did you heal him?" He rested his hand on the nape of Alvix's neck, stroking the sensitive spot behind his ear lightly.

"I figured out the hard way that my fire can heal as well as destroy." Alvix leaned into Cooper's touch. "It hurts either way, so I tend not to use it at all."

Pope's eyes fluttered open, and Cooper steeled himself not to show his discomfort at the change in Pope's eye color. Before the Tongassians tortured him, Pope's eyes were completely brown. Now they had gold streaks racing through them like flickering flames. Pope frowned when he saw Alvix and Cooper in the room with him.

"Wasn't the doctor here?" His destroyed voice still grated on Cooper, but it sounded better than it had when they first got to Tative.

"Yes, but he had to leave in a hurry." Cooper frowned.

"He cut me with something, I think." Pope pinned Alvix with his gaze. "You saved us."

Alvix grimaced. "Trust me, I was as surprised as you when I offered."

A grin skated across Pope's face. "I bet. You don't strike me as the sacrificing type."

"You wouldn't think it to look at me."

General Gateway burst through the door. "Alexander, are you okay?"

Alvix and Cooper moved out of the way, letting the general get to his son. Cooper dropped his hand from Alvix's neck, resting it at the small of his back instead.

"I'm fine, or at least, I think I am now." His eyes skipped over to Alvix before looking back at his father.

The general looked at Alvix, who nodded. Taking a deep breath, Gateway patted his son on the shoulder before gesturing for Cooper to follow him. "Lieutenant Cooper and I have a meeting scheduled. He can tell me what happened here. Captain Alvix, are you here to visit Alexander?"

"If he allows it, sir. I won't force my company on anyone." Alvix smiled at Pope.

"Alexander?" The general asked his son.

"It's fine with me, Father. I'd like to talk to Captain Alvix."

"Good. Lieutenant Cooper will come and retrieve you when we're finished." Gateway stalked from the room.

"Retrieve me like I'm a piece of space garbage," Alvix mumbled loud enough for Cooper to hear.

Cooper pinched Alvix's firm ass. "Stop. He didn't mean it that way, and you know it."

"Get out of here before he comes back to retrieve you." Alvix winked and laughed.

He didn't want the general to come after him, considering the mood the man was in. He raced from the room to catch him.

CHAPTER 10

Alvix stared after Cooper until Pope cleared his throat. Turning back to the corporal, he shrugged apologetically.

::What can I say? I'm a sucker for a tight ass.::

Pope rolled his eyes and held out a hand. *::Help me sit up. I hate lying flat on my back.::*

He got the young soldier propped up with pillows and a glass of water in hand. Pulling a chair up next to the bed, he flopped into it, then swung his feet up on the bed, making sure not to hit Pope with them.

Pushing the blankets off, Pope shook his head. *::Everyone insists on covering me with blankets, but I'm hotter than hell, even without them::*

::It's the fire.::

The confusion on Pope's face was why Alvix wanted to talk to him. He leaned forward and tapped the man's hand. *::Don't worry. I'll help you through this.::*

"Through what?" Worry started edging out confusion as Pope spoke out loud. Shock sparked in the soldier's eyes. "Were we talking in our heads?"

Alvix shoved his hand through his hair and sighed. "Unfortunately, you absorbed enough Tongassian fire to change you in fundamental ways. One of which is that you and I now have a link through the fire."

"What are you talking about?" Pope shifted, gripping the glass in his hand tight enough to make his knuckles go white.

"The Tongassians are formed from fire. They are living, breathing flames and, because of that, their fire is different."

He studied his hands, loosening his control a little to let the flame dance along his fingertips. It was mesmerizing, flickering and skipping without burning or marking his flesh.

"I thought you ate fire." Pope stared at him.

"Oh, I have many talents. Eating fire is just one of them. I can create fire out of thin air, though that takes more energy than I like to expend. And hell, you'd never need heavy blankets during the cold seasons because I'm just as good as a heater."

Pope picked at the blankets. "Is that why I can't stand having a blanket on?"

"You'll always be warmer than a normal person now, but it'll settle down once your body has recovered." He closed his hand and snuffed the flames out.

"I won't be like you, will I?" Pope grimaced. "I hope you're not offended by that."

Alvix snorted. "Of course, you won't be like me. I'm unique, I think. If there are any more like me out there, I haven't met them. Those I knew about are gone."

He pushed to his feet and paced. How did he get Pope to talk to him about what had happened? He'd never tried to be friends with anyone. Never cared enough about anyone to listen to their problems.

"Why'd you do it?"

Pausing in mid-stride, he glanced over at Pope. "Do what?"

"Why did you trade yourself for us?"

Honesty seemed like the best policy. Alvix shrugged. "I don't know."

Pope didn't look convinced. "No one does something like that on a whim."

"You wouldn't think so, would you? All I know was, I entered the throne room and you were burning. Maybe I wanted to repay a debt."

The kid shuddered. A friend probably wouldn't bring up bad memories, but Alvix knew there was no point in beating around the proverbial bush. Pope had been tortured and the man was never going to forget that.

"I know how that feels. I've had that happen to me a time or two before." He paced over to the window and stared out.

Pope's room overlooked an empty area of the yard. Rivers, Steele, Callum, and a fourth man Alvix assumed was Apple punched and kicked each other.

"You have very loyal and determined friends." Alvix turned and leaned against the windowsill, his arms folded across his chest.

"We learned the hard way we could only trust each other." Pope grimaced. "Most of the places we're sent, we don't have back-up coming to save our asses."

Alvix studied the floor under his boots. "I also knew I could survive whatever that Tongassian did to me. My body's hard-wired to absorb fire and heat. None of you would have survived very long."

"Because we're human, and you're not."

"Right."

"What the fuck are you then?"

His head shot up at Cooper's harsh demand. Pope lifted a shoulder, as if to say he didn't know Cooper had entered the room.

Rubbing his jaw, Alvix returned his gaze to the floor, organizing his thoughts. He wasn't sure how to explain what he was.

"Are you Tongassian?" Cooper stalked farther into the room.

"If I was, would the king have tortured me?" He controlled the urge to roll his eyes.

"We only saw him attack you while we were there. How do we know what happened after we left?"

His brittle laughter filled the air. "Right. I endured rape and fire to convince you I wasn't a bad guy. And I would accomplish what with that plan?"

"LT." Pope tried to interrupt. Maybe he could guess at what was going to happen.

"Maybe you're a Tongassian spy."

"The Tongassians don't care about you, GalMil, or anything outside of their planet. They also don't have the ability to disguise their true nature." Alvix glared at Cooper.

Cooper propped his fists on his hips and disbelief flared in his eyes. Was last night a charming interlude between them or would Cooper be willing to accept that Alvix told the truth as he knew it?

"You could be part of the scheme to hurt Pope and betray General Gateway."

"Now you're just grasping at straws." He marched up to Cooper and poked him in the chest. "You came to *me.* You made me take you to that fucking planet. I didn't have to trade myself for you. I could've let you all fry."

Alvix closed his eyes and cleared his throat. "Trust me, there were times when I asked myself why I did it."

Opening his eyes, he gazed up at Cooper and saw the struggle the man was fighting to believe Alvix. He placed two fingers on Cooper's temples.

"I can share my memories with you. It'll hurt and won't be pleasant, but it might help you believe me."

Alvix didn't really want to do it, but he couldn't think of any other way. His scars had healed to the point they were mere white lines on his body. He had no wounds to show for his month bathing in flame.

"Do it."

The fire simmering deep inside Alvix surged and he let a small amount out. Orange tendrils connected his fingers to Cooper's head. Sweat beaded on the man's metal skin.

"LT, no." Pope struggled to climb out of bed.

"It's all right." Cooper ground his teeth together.

The place where they touched grew white hot, and Alvix allowed his memories to flow along their link. He kept the link between him and Pope blocked.

Cooper twitched and jerked as Alvix's torture played out in his mind. They reached the point of Alvix's disembowelment, and Cooper tore away from him, hunched over, and gagged.

Alvix poured a glass of water and held it out to Cooper, who grabbed it, draining the glass in two large gulps.

Pope narrowed his eyes at Alvix. "You didn't have to do that to him."

"I warned him." Alvix took up his station by the window again.

"What kind of creature are you to survive all that without dying?" Cooper slumped into the chair Alvix abandoned earlier.

Placing his hand on the window, his skin steamed encountering the chilly surface. "We have no real name. Others called us fire-eaters, and we've accepted it. For that is what we are, sort of."

"Where do you come from?" Pope sounded intrigued.

"There isn't one planet we call home. A dying star creates us. Our essence or being is ejected as the star collapses inward and we travel through the universe."

Cooper frowned, seemingly listening and trying to make sense of what Alvix was saying. "How many of you exist?"

"I don't know. Of the group I became a part of, only I live now, but there could be others all over the universe on planets you know nothing about."

CHAPTER 11

Cooper stared at the man standing in the room with him and Pope. He looked like Alvix and sounded like him, but the cold distance in his voice and manner knocked Cooper off-center. Where had this other Alvix been hiding?

He looked over at Pope, who shrugged when their eyes met.

"Is this your true form or a disguise?"

"If I were to take my true form, I'd destroy this planet."

"Okay, we don't need to see that." He held up his hands.

Alvix flashed him a grin. "I didn't think so."

"You pretend to be human?" Cooper was trying to organize all the new information in his mind.

"Yes, and for the most part, I am exactly what you see before you. I really am a barely-scraping-by transport pilot who, somehow, managed to be a hero for once in his life."

"It's only when you're around fire that your secret is revealed." Pope looked like he accepted what Alvix said.

Alvix nodded. "The very core of my being is fire. Yours is water. Too much exposure to fire would kill you. I knew it, insuring I had no choice except to take your place with the king."

"Why didn't you escape? Something tells me you're way more powerful than the Tongassians."

Cooper stood, compelled by some emotion he didn't really want to examine, to go to Alvix. Reaching out, he rested his hand on Alvix's back between his shoulder blades. A tremor tore through Alvix, but he didn't move away.

"My power has been under wraps for as long as I've been cognizant. Losing control could prove to be deadly for everyone around me. I've never used it to save myself." He glanced over his shoulder at Cooper. "If I could have, don't you think I would've used it to get away from Weldon, instead of relying on my intelligence?"

The man had a point and Cooper nodded in silent acknowledgement of it. The door burst open and the other four members of Cooper's team tumbled in.

Rivers and Steele wrestled, while Callum cheered them on. Apple stood a few feet away, his face expressionless, but tension obvious in every line of his body.

"Stop it," Cooper ordered.

All the men snapped to attention, gazes facing straight ahead.

"What were you fighting about this time?"

"Nothing, LT." Rivers' grin informed Cooper he'd never find out either.

None of his guys ratted each other out. It was that loyalty that made him sure their betrayer was from outside their unit.

"You see, I understand the concepts of loyalty, compassion, and sacrifice, but I never got to put them to use until I met you. Compassion and loyalty are admirable traits." Alvix's voice was low enough only Cooper could hear.

"What about sacrifice?"

"Highly over-rated and really actually sucks." Alvix patted Cooper's ass before sauntering toward the door. "I'll leave you gentlemen to your top secret discussion. I'm going to find something to eat."

Cooper frowned. Whatever odd personality quirk Alvix had been channeling seemed gone, or else Alvix could turn it on and off at will. He had to remember something else lurked under that rather benign façade.

"Interesting man, LT." Butter wouldn't melt in Pope's mouth.

"Yes, he is." Giving himself a mental shake, Cooper got back on track. "Sit." He sat in the chair next to Pope's bed.

Steele claimed a spot on the bed. Rivers stood near one of the windows, and Apple edged closer to the door, looking like he'd bolt at the slightest sound. Callum stayed near Apple.

"The general passed along our new orders. We're to meet up with a platoon of infantry just out of the Singer Galaxy. There's been a coup on one of their planets and they're requesting GalMil assistance."

"Bad move. Once the GalMil gets a foot in that galaxy, they won't be leaving." Rivers spoke aloud what the rest of them were thinking.

"When do we leave?" Steele laid a hand on Pope's blanket-covered knee.

"As soon as preparations are done. Rivers, I need you and Callum to coordinate with Jensen. She'll get us re-supplied with ammo and weapons. Steele, get whatever information you can on the Singer Galaxy and its inhabitants. I'm not sure which planet we're going to hit."

"What about Apple and me, LT?" Pope waved a hand at the other soldier.

"I'm afraid you're not going with us, Pope. You're still recovering, and the doctors aren't confident Apple won't flip out on us."

He held up his hand before either Pope or Callum could do more than take a breath. Apple didn't react.

"Both of you need more time to heal. You especially, Pope, now you don't have the nano-mites to help you out. Don't think you're getting off easy, though. I want you to keep an eye on Alvix." He caught Apple's gaze, forcing the man to acknowledge him.

"Apple, I need you to be Alvix's shadow. Make sure all of the doctors and scientists stay away from him." Cooper looked at Pope after Apple nodded. "Pope, be his friend for now. He can help you recover and deal with what happened to you. Your father is also making plans for him. Wherever he goes, I want you two to go with him. Don't worry. We'll find you when our mission is over."

Pope stayed silent, but inclined his head in agreement. Apple didn't as much as grimace, which wasn't unusual since they got back from Tongass, and Cooper hated it. Apple had never been as extroverted or upbeat as Callum, but at least he'd talked. Now they couldn't get him to say a word or show any emotion.

Cooper wasn't sure about leaving the younger men in charge of keeping Alvix safe, but it wasn't his call. The general thought it would be easy work for them both while they were recovering.

Gateway could be right. Alvix was more than capable of taking care of himself, if one believed all that bullshit about being born of a dead star.

"We get to babysit the crazy man while you go kick some ass. Just like little kids being sent to hide when bad things are going to happen," Pope muttered.

Steele stroked his knee. "Hey, kid, you're not ready to go back into combat. Without the nano-mites, you're as vulnerable as the next human, and if you get injured, you could die. We're not ready to get rid of you yet."

Pope stared at Steele, and Cooper made a mental note to ask the sergeant what was going on between the two of them.

"Fine, but we'll be waiting for you." Pope glanced at Apple. "Won't we?"

Apple's expression didn't change, but Cooper noticed a slight tilt to Apple's head.

"Good. Once I find out for sure what the general has in store for Alvix, I'll give you your orders. Until then, the rest of us need to get ready for the mission."

"What about whoever set us up?" Rivers snarled with contempt.

He'd wondered when someone was going to bring that up. "General Gateway has others in higher positions looking into it for us. When the time comes, we'll deploy to deal with it. Trust me, the general isn't going to leave us hanging."

His teammates signaled their approval with salutes.

"Apple, can you sweep Alvix's room for bugs?"

"You think someone's spying on him, LT?" Callum spoke for Apple.

"Let's just say I wouldn't put it past the scientists to study him without his permission." He snapped his fingers. "That reminds me. Doctor Leonoid has been relieved of duty here and will be re-assigned elsewhere."

Pope ran a finger over the scar on his wrist. "Probably a good idea."

"My thoughts exactly." Cooper stood. "Get moving, gentlemen. Our official orders will be arriving soon."

They saluted as Cooper left. He paused in the hallway, working out in his mind where he might find Alvix.

"Lieutenant."

One of the guards approached him.

"Yes, Corporal?"

"Captain Alvix is in the garden, sir, if you were looking for him."

"Thank you."

He headed for the garden, admitting he should have thought of that first.

CHAPTER12

Face raised to the bright sun, Alvix soaked up the warmth. There was something pure about sunlight. Maybe, like a fish needed water to survive, Alvix needed the sunlight or warmth to continue.

"Would you care to join me?"

"How'd you know I was here?" Cooper sounded disgruntled.

Peeking through his eyelashes, the angle of Cooper's head showed Alvix the officer's confusion.

"The sound of the wind changed when you got near, plus I could smell you. You have an oddly intriguing scent of oil and male." He opened his eyes fully at Cooper's snort. "Not buying any of that?"

Cooper shook his head.

"All right. You're casting a shadow on me. Happens when you stand in the sun. It got cool." He motioned to the bench he sat on. "Would you like to sit?"

Starting to pace, Cooper traversed the path in front of Alvix. "Is all that shit about being created from a dying star true?"

"You can't just accept it on blind faith?" He chuckled.

"I'm a soldier."

Like that explained everything.

"I feel the need to point out that most soldiers are expected to obey orders without questions." He closed his eyes and leaned his head back, keeping track of Cooper by his footsteps, now that he wasn't trying to sneak up on Alvix anymore.

"You're right, but even a soldier would find your story too far-fetched to accept without some doubt."

"True." He lifted a shoulder. "It's a good story, isn't it? I can't tell you whether it's true or not. My first memory is picking pockets for money to put in the communal kitty. The adults used it to buy food and supplies for the rest of us."

"Where were your parents?"

"I don't know. I don't even remember anyone claiming me. When I asked one of the adults, they told me that story. It made more sense to a five-year-old who could light things on fire with a thought to believe he was born from a dying star than to believe he's a freak."

"But when you got older, I'm sure they told you the truth."

"What's the truth?" Alvix opened his eyes and stared down at his hands, allowing a small amount of fire to spark along his fingers. "They never changed their story, no matter how many times I asked. I finally decided to stop asking and accept that inside their fanciful story was probably a kernel of truth."

Cooper stayed quiet for a little while, and Alvix didn't speak, not wanting to talk about his past anymore.

"Do *you* really believe you were created from a star?" Cooper stopped in front of him and challenged him.

"Aside from the Tongassians, how many species do you know of who can create fire? Any species that absorb fire without being burnt to ashes?"

"None," Cooper admitted.

Alvix snuffed out the flames on his pants and let his hands rest in his lap. "None and, as far as I know, I'm the only one left. I'm not Tongassian because they could never hold a human form like I can."

The soldier scuffed his boot in the dirt. "Haven't you ever wondered about your parents?"

"Not really. I was trying to survive and didn't have time to worry about who or where they were." Alvix shot a quick glance at Cooper. "What about your parents? After they abandoned you to the military, did you ever try finding them?"

Pacing resumed. It seemed like Cooper didn't want to discuss his parents either. Alvix didn't mind Cooper's silence. It was better they didn't get attached to each other more than they already were.

Cooper would be recalled and his unit sent on another dangerous mission, while, after a few days, Alvix would be escorted to the nearest space stop and left. General Gateway would give him a generous reward, he was sure, but nothing else, and Alvix didn't expect more than that.

"I did go looking for them. Had a friend search the GalMil's personnel files. Even though any kid given to the academy is listed as an orphan, the GalMil keeps tabs on the parents, just in case they haven't really cut all the apron strings."

Standing, Alvix grabbed Cooper's hand and dragged him down one of the garden walkways. He had a specific place in mind. A place he'd found earlier while he wandered outside. Cooper didn't ask about their destination because his focus was on his past.

"My friend found that the last mention of them was when I was ten. A GalMil officer went to talk to them and ensure they weren't going to come and claim me again."

He stumbled a bit, but Alvix didn't slow down.

"They had two other kids and disavowed any knowledge of me. As far as they were concerned, I didn't exist."

"Shit, man. That sucks." Alvix meant that. He never knew his parents; had no memories to make their desertion hurt more.

"It is what it is."

Cooper sounded fine with what happened. Alvix figured the man had never really gotten over his parents' abandonment.

"Where are you taking me?"

It was good to see memories hadn't taken all of Cooper's attention. Alvix flashed a "trust me" smile over his shoulder at Cooper before ducking through a large hedge. He pushed branches aside, chuckling at the grunts behind him as some errant sticks hit Cooper.

"Don't worry. It's no place bad. Just a spot I discovered."

They broke through the hedge and he stopped, sweeping his free arm out. "Look."

Cooper stumbled to a halt next to him, and Alvix grinned as the man's mouth fell open.

Whoever had designed the grounds around the house deserved a medal or lots of money. They'd found the perfect balance between stimulating the senses and encouraging peace. The clearing was a shining example of the best of the gardens.

All varieties of flowers blossomed in riotous colors, spreading drunkenly across the space, yet somehow guiding a person to the pool at the far side. The water reflected the blueness of the sky and puffy whiteness of the clouds. At one end of the pool, a small waterfall laughed and cascaded its way down rocks to land in the pool with a joyful splash.

"Wow," Cooper whispered.

Alvix watched as weight seemed to life from Cooper's shoulders and years rolled off his body. He left Cooper standing there and practically skipped his way to the pool. He thought he heard a snicker coming from Cooper's direction, but when he glanced back, the man appeared to be studying the waterfall intently.

He shrugged, not caring how silly he looked. The colors and freedom took him back to being a child, or as child-like as he could ever be, having never really been a kid.

"What are you doing?"

Pausing, he looked up to find Cooper watching him. "I'm going swimming."

"Naked?"

Why did Cooper sound shocked?

"Surprisingly, my wardrobe isn't varied enough to include swim trunks." He tugged off his boots and stripped out of his pants, underwear, and socks all at once. Cooper's eyes widened for a moment when Alvix straightened.

"Are you embarrassed?" Alvix swallowed his laughter. "You've seen me naked before. Hell, you let me rub off on you."

Cooper shifted, but didn't reply. Alvix wandered over to the pool, dipping a toe into the water. For most people, the temperature would be tepid. For him, it was cool.

"Are there any native creatures that you should be worried about?" Cooper drew closer.

Shaking his head, Alvix contemplated jumping in or easing inch by inch until he was up to his chest.

"I talked to the gardener. There's nothing in this particular pond. It's all man-made and fed from the water system connected to the house."

Not knowing how deep the pool was made up Alvix's mind. After sitting, he slipped into the chilly water and bit back the groan wanting to escape from his throat. He ducked under the water and soaked his hair, swimming to where the waterfall merged with the surface of the pool.

When he arrived there, he broke the surface and allowed the water to trickle down his body. Alvix turned, sweeping his hair out of his face.

Cooper stood on the bank, studying him with those eerie eyes.

"Can you get wet without rusting?" Alvix pitched his voice to ensure Cooper heard him over the falling liquid.

"Yes, I can. How do you think I keep clean?" Cooper glared at him.

He shrugged and lifted his hand to watch the sparkling droplets drip from his fingers. "Guess I figured if you got dirty, you just wiped yourself off like I would my ship."

Cooper snorted, and Alvix wiped his hand across his face to hide his smile.

"I'm not a machine."

Peering through wet locks of hair, Alvix stared while Cooper stripped, to his eternal delight. Cooper seemed to be assessing the pros and cons of entering when he paused at the pond's edge while Alvix enjoyed the view.

Cooper was tall and very muscular, as a highly trained soldier should be. His six-pack abs were sharply defined and Alvix bit his lip, wanting to ask if the nano-mites created the chiseled look or did the little robots only enhance what was there naturally.

He visually devoured Cooper's cock as it stiffened and rose from the nest of dark curls at the man's groin. He swam over when Cooper stepped into the pond.

Alvix grasped Cooper's hips and flashed the man a quick grin before he surrounded the crown of Cooper's prick with his lips, applying enough pressure to drag a groan from Cooper. Kneeling on the sandy bottom of the pond, he slowly worked his way down until the spongy head of Cooper's cock hit the back of his throat.

"Damn, Alvix."

He hummed and a shudder wracked Cooper's body. Cooper buried his hands in Alvix's hair, flexing his fingers to the point of pain, but Alvix didn't protest. He was too busy, swallowing the hot liquid spilling from Cooper's prick. When the last drops slipped down his throat, he licked Cooper clean and allowed the softened flesh to slide from his mouth, dropping a gentle kiss on the head.

Cooper patted his head, and Alvix caught the man as his knees gave out. He lowered Cooper to the edge of the pond. While Cooper recovered his strength, Alvix swam. The cool water soothed him as much as Cooper's touch did. He'd always been more of a water child than fire. Maybe it was because the fire formed his core, never allowing him to get away from it.

"Why?"

Glancing over his shoulder, he spied Cooper in the same spot, leaning back on his hands and legs dangling in the water. The man stared at him with a quizzical tilt to his head.

"Why what?" He flipped over, floating on his back, enjoying the brush of his hair against his skin.

"Why the sex?" Cooper frowned. "It's not because you're grateful to me for saving you, is it?"

Alvix laughed. "Well, I am grateful you came back to rescue me, but I don't do gratitude sex, or pity fucks for that matter. I'm attracted to you and I actually like you. As long as you're interested, why not get our rocks off with each other? It's not like either of us expects the other to fall in love."

Cooper looked down. "What if one of us does fall in love?"

"Are you saying you love me, Cooper?" Alvix swam over to where Cooper still studied the water in front of him.

Sighing, Cooper scrubbed a hand over his mouth and shrugged. "I don't know what to call how I feel for you, Alvix. I mean, we just met again a couple of months ago. At which time, I promptly got you taken prisoner by a psychotic flame king and abandoned you to all kinds of torture."

"So what you could be feeling is simple guilt." He rested his hand on Cooper's knee. "You're a good man, no matter how hard you try to convince me that you're tough and unfeeling. I wish I could get you to accept the fact you don't have to feel guilty for anything. I made the choice to change places with you. Your unit does more good in this universe than I can flying transports."

"I'm not sure how much good my unit actually does. We invade planets that don't want us there. We take away their freedoms and force them to become a part of the GalMil. How is that good?"

Okay, so Cooper had a point there. Alvix stroked his thumb over Cooper's thigh as he thought. Finally, he admitted, "I'm not sure what good that does, but still you came back for me and no one's ever done that for me."

He ducked down to meet Cooper's gaze. Alvix wanted to insure the man understood how sincere he was.

"What I feel for you has nothing to do with gratitude. I like you, Cooper. If we had the time, maybe it could've been more, but we don't have time to see where this could take us."

Cooper didn't look completely convinced, but Alvix didn't know how to make the man understand he didn't do anything like that. Alvix had sex because he wanted to, for the most part. Not because he felt obligated or anything like that. When Alvix chose to have sex, it was because he liked the person he was going to bed with.

There seemed to be a little more chivalrous knight in Cooper than the guy wanted to admit. Surging up, Alvix kissed Cooper hard.

"Try not to worry about it too much. It'll all work out somehow." He pulled himself out of the water. "We should probably head back."

CHAPTER 13

As they dressed, Cooper kept his gaze on his clothes and away from Alvix's ass. If he stared too long, he'd be tempted to grab those firm cheeks and they'd have another go there in the grass.

Those urges and the utter lack of self-control Cooper felt when he was around Alvix weren't very professional. He feared his conduct would reach the ear of General Gateway, who would reprimand him for it.

::We're technically on leave, LT.:: Steele's words echoed in his head. *::No one cares what you do.::*

::Do me a favor, Steele. While you're looking up information for the mission, see what you can find on Captain Alvix and fire-eaters.:: He buttoned his pants and reached for his socks.

::Sure thing, but I bet most of what I find about the fire-eaters will be rumors and myths.::

Tugging on his socks, he gave a mental shrug. *::I won't take that bet. I'm pretty sure with enough lies, we can pick out a few kernels of truth and figure out what the hell Alvix is.::*

::That's a possibility, sir.:: Steele didn't sound confident.

::Just do it, please.::

He glanced up and found Alvix standing near the break in the hedge they'd come through, dressed and waiting for Cooper. He snatched up his shirt and slipped it on as he strolled toward Alvix.

"Done talking to your man?"

If he could blush, he'd be beet red. "How did you know I was talking to one of them?"

"I'm linked to Pope through our connection to fire. I only know if you're communicating with them. I have no idea what you're talking about."

::Thank God.::

Laughter filled his head.

"Forgot something I needed done," he muttered and pushed passed Alvix.

The other man didn't say a word, merely followed him back to the house.

Jensen called to them as they stepped inside. "Captain Alvix, the general would like to see you at your earliest convenience."

Alvix's eyes narrowed, and Cooper waited to see if Alvix was going to say no. Should he warn him it wasn't wise to tell a supreme general no?

"Would you be willing to bring me some food?" Alvix inquired, charming Jensen with a smile.

She nodded. "Certainly. General Gateway said you are welcome to come as well, Lieutenant."

He hesitated, unsure how Alvix felt about him attending the meeting. Alvix waved his hand for Jensen to lead the way.

"You might as well come along. You'll find out what was said eventually."

Cooper couldn't argue with that, so he followed them. They wound their way through corridors and rooms. They had to be going to the general's private study. He'd only been to the main conference room, never anywhere near Gateway's personal quarters.

Two soldiers guarded the door. They saluted when they approached, and one opened it for them.

"Sergeant Jensen to see you, sir," the soldier announced them.

"Let them in."

Jensen and Alvix entered, while Cooper hung back, surprised at the general's rather informal dress. Gateway wore simple black pants and a light knit shirt. His feet were bare and his usually neatly styled hair stood up in places as if he'd been running his fingers through it.

"Good, you brought Cooper. It saves me from sending you for him."

After waving them in, Gateway nodded to a pair of chairs and a couch situated in front of an empty fireplace. Jensen took one chair while the general sat in the other, leaving the couch for Cooper and

Alvix.

He sat, trying not to get too close to Alvix. It was bad enough that the heat radiating from him seemed to call to Cooper, but Cooper's body took a great deal of interest in how Alvix smelled. They'd just finished having sex thirty minutes ago. He shouldn't be that interested in going again, especially in the presence of his commanding officer.

Cooper might not be ashamed of who he spent his personal time with, but that was private and not for public consumption. No matter how informal the meeting with General Gateway was, the man was still a higher-ranking soldier, and Cooper wasn't going to relax because of that.

"Remember when I asked you what you wanted as a reward for saving my son?" the general asked with a raised brow.

"Yes, sir." Alvix leaned forward slightly, gaze pinned on Gateway.

"Normally, any Earth land is passed from father to son and only the richest families can afford it."

Confusion wrinkled Alvix's brow. "What are you talking about?"

Gateway frowned. "Of course, if you know someone who happens to have connections, you might be lucky."

Pope's father seemed frustrated yet very pleased with himself. What had happened since the last time Cooper had talked to the general?

"I'm not very good with hints. Maybe you should just tell me what the hell you're trying to say." Alvix vibrated next to Cooper.

"An old friend of mine has no son to inherit the ancestral home and he's dying. I approached him with my proposal, which he accepted." Gateway stood, wandered over to his desk, and picked a thin file off a pile of folders.

"What sort of proposal, sir?" Cooper cringed inside when all three sets of eyes met his. He hadn't meant to ask that out loud.

"I suggested he consider making Alvix his heir. He really doesn't have any family left." Gateway paused a moment before continuing. "No one would know who you are and with his permission, you could hide on Earth for a while."

A look of dawning comprehension lit Alvix's face, while Cooper's gut tightened. Something had happened.

"Why do I need to hide?"

For the first time since Cooper met the general, Gateway looked uncomfortable.

"Unfortunately, it seems that, even though Doctor Leonoid was re-assigned and sworn to secrecy, he talked to a few people in the scientific branch of GalMil."

Alvix stiffened, and Cooper growled. They should have wiped Leonoid's memory clean or done something to ensure he couldn't tell anyone about Alvix.

"Now the scientists want me brought in for study like I'm some strange, as yet undetermined, species." Alvix bared his clenched his teeth. "That'll never happen."

Before Gateway could say anything, Cooper jumped in. "Of course, it won't. We won't allow them to put a finger on you. You're part of our unit now, and we take care of our own."

The raised eyebrow and doubt-filled look Alvix gave him conveyed the man's skepticism more than any words could.

"That's why Apple and Alexander are going with you." Cooper nodded as Gateway glanced at him. "I already informed the men they were to travel with Captain Alvix wherever he went."

"Without asking me?" Alvix's eyes flashed with annoyance.

"Yes, without asking. I'm sure you're used to taking care of yourself, Alvix, but having someone around to watch your back is important." Cooper leaned back on the couch and folded his arms over his chest. "There's no discussion about them going with you."

Alvix jumped to his feet and paced, while glancing at the general. "Don't take this wrong, but how the hell is Pope going to keep me safe?"

Gateway's rueful expression spoke volumes. "You're right, but I think giving both of them the responsibility of keeping you safe might help them recover faster."

"To do what? Now that the nano-mites were destroyed inside Pope, he won't ever become invulnerable. He's always going to have that strange patchwork look to him. There's no reversing it, and re-injecting them won't work either. Pope's always going to have an affinity for fire, so his body will burn them out."

Cooper and the general both grimaced. They had discussed that possibility, but the consensus was they would do everything they could to keep Pope in the unit.

"He's a soldier, whether he stays in my unit or gets transferred elsewhere. He'll do his job." Cooper had all the confidence in Pope doing his duty, no matter what happened.

"Ah, yes, because there isn't anything better than being a soldier."

Cooper didn't let the sarcasm dripping from Alvix's words insult him. Those who had never been in the military didn't understand how important it became to the men and women who served.

"I have a life. It might not seem like much of one to you, but it was mine."

Cooper, Jensen, and Gateway watched Alvix pace, and Cooper struggled to keep from promising that everything would be fine. That Alvix wouldn't have to hide out forever, but he knew better and Alvix wouldn't appreciate him blowing smoke up his ass either.

"Once we get to Earth, what am I supposed to do? I'm a transport pilot, not some lazy-ass rich man who never did a minute of work in my life." Alvix directed the question toward Gateway.

The general shrugged. "I'm sure you'll find something. While you are there, Captain Alvix, you won't have to worry about money or anything."

Alvix continued to pace, running his hands through his hair with frustrated jerks. "How are you going to explain my disappearance?"

"You must have been getting suspicious, so you snuck away in the middle of the night."

"With your son and one of his team mates? No one's going to buy that, not even from a supreme general."

Gateway stood. "We'll deal with it when we come to that question. I want you to leave tonight. Jensen will make sure your ship has fuel and the coordinates you need to land on Earth. I will make sure all your papers are in order. They'll be waiting for you onboard. There will probably be a welcoming committee when you land, so read up on the background information of the family you've become a part of."

Alvix looked like he wanted to argue some more, but Cooper knew when a conference was over. He stood and saluted the general. "I'll make sure Captain Alvix and the corporals are ready."

"Good. I'll send Jensen for you when it's time."

"Thank you, sir."

Cooper grabbed Alvix's hand and dragged the man from the room. Alvix didn't protest or fight him, but Cooper could see unhappiness in every line of Alvix's body. He just hoped Alvix would wait until they got back to his set of rooms before he said anything.

Alvix flung himself into a chair when they reached his room. Cooper leaned against the door, staring at his lover.

"I don't want to do this. Why can't I just take my ship and leave?"

"The GalMil wants you, Alvix, and they'll do whatever they must to get you. The general is doing what he can to keep you safe. You helped save his son. He owes you since that situation brought you to the GalMil's attention."

"No one owes me anything." Alvix's frustration showed in the harshness of his voice. "I keep trying to tell you all that."

Cooper strolled over and crouched in front of Alvix. "You might be used to no one caring for you or admitting they were wrong when they do something to hurt you."

"What have you done to hurt me?"

"By not really giving you a choice about this whole matter. If you don't go on your own, the general will bind you and toss you on your ship with orders to Pope and Apple to take you to Earth."

Alvix sighed and leaned forward, resting his forehead against Cooper's. "Will you come to Earth?"

"As soon as our mission is complete, I'll be flying in. I'm sure I won't be alone either."

"Steele and Callum will be with you as well." Alvix guessed.

"Yeah. I'm getting the feeling there's more going on between my men than I imagined." He closed his eyes, breathing in Alvix's scent.

"Facing death every day can forge very close personal ties between men." Alvix chuckled.

Cooper stood and held out his hand to Alvix. "Let's head to bed. I have a feeling Jensen will be showing up in the middle of the night."

Alvix seemed to recognize the futility of arguing any more. He took Cooper's hand and allowed him to pull him to his feet.

Ten minutes later, they stood in Alvix's room, staring at each other. Cooper's silver eyes met his, and Alvix understood it could be the last time they ever saw each other. He didn't want to leave without having Cooper inside him.

Walking forward, he didn't stop until he pressed as tightly as he could to Cooper's chest. He slipped his arms around Cooper's shoulders and smiled.

::Make love to me.::

Cooper jumped, seemingly surprised Alvix would chose to communicate mind-to-mind. He nuzzled along Alvix's jaw line. *::Are you sure?::*

Nodding, Alvix rocked their pelvises hips together. *::Yes. I know the difference between what the Tongassian king did to me and what will happen between us. I want to have at least one memory of your cock in my ass before we're separated.::*

::Geesh, you're so romantic.::

::It's a gift.::

85

Enough talk. Alvix stepped back, dragging Cooper with him until the back of his knees hit the edge of the mattress. When they halted, he broke contact and proceeded to strip, tossing his clothes in every direction, not caring where they landed. Cooper bared his own body just as quickly.

They tumbled onto the bed in a tangle of limbs, mouths devouring each other like it was the last few seconds of time they'd have together. Alvix shuddered, accepting deep inside the fact that it probably was. He pushed all those thoughts away, sinking into the coolness bathing his body where Cooper's skin touched his.

He sighed into Cooper's mouth as the larger man covered him from chest to knee like a heavy metal blanket. Their cocks rubbed together, and he arched, eager to get Cooper inside him. Letting his head fall back, Alvix slid his hands down Cooper's back to grab his ass and grip the firm muscles there.

"Please fuck me," he begged.

"I need to get you ready."

Cooper reared back and placed his fingers on Alvix's lips. Alvix sucked them in, bathing them with his spit, and getting them good and wet. When salvia dripped from his mouth, down Cooper's hand, Cooper removed his fingers and spread Alvix's thighs.

Grabbing hold of his thighs behind his knees, Alvix pulled his legs wide, giving Cooper better access to his hole.

"Don't take too long. I really want you in me and I don't care about the pain."

"But I don't want to hurt you." Cooper pressed one finger in Alvix's hole, drawing a low moan from Alvix.

"You can't hurt me. Do it quick."

His lover took him at his word and within a minute, three digits stretched the tight ring of muscles guarding Alvix's inner passage.

Each push in nailed Alvix's gland and shot electricity through his body. He shivered and trembled, rocking up to meet those thick columns of flesh. His gaze fixed on Cooper's face and the fierce look of concentration Cooper wore.

"Now," he ordered. Any more riding and he'd spill before Cooper ever got into him.

Cooper spit into his hand and coated his cock with salvia. Alvix spread his legs farther apart as Cooper settled between them and positioned the head of his prick at Alvix's opening.

Their groans mingled as Cooper drove in, not stopping until he was buried balls deep in Alvix's ass. Alvix hissed and bit his lip, absorbing the burn of Cooper's invasion and trying to breathe through it. Cooper froze above him, not willing to move. Alvix blinked, and relaxed as the pain mutated into pleasure. He clenched his inner muscles and tilted his hips slightly, giving Cooper the signal he waited for.

Soon all thought of anything except Cooper's fat dick plunging in and out of him left Alvix's mind. He became entranced with the rhythm they established and how marvelously their bodies moved together. He fought the urge to close his eyes as his climax built. He wanted to remember how Cooper looked surging into him time and time again.

Pressure pooled in his lower back and his balls drew close to his body. The pleasure abyss drew closer and he fisted his hands into the sheets under him.

"I'm close," he warned Cooper.

"Good," Cooper grunted out. "So am I."

Three hard, fast thrusts, each one hitting Alvix's gland, put him over and his cum shot from his cock to coat his stomach and chest. As his inner channel clamped down on Cooper's cock, his lover cried out, flooding Alvix's ass with Cooper's own hot seed.

They shuddered and quaked together, drawing out their mutual climaxes as long as possible. Finally, Cooper's strength gave out and the man collapsed on top of Alvix. Their panting sounded loud in the dark room. Alvix stroked his hands down Cooper's sweat-covered back while they calmed their heartbeats down.

"Where are you going?" he asked as Cooper climbed off him and out of bed.

"To get a cloth to clean you up with."

Having a lover take care of him was a novel idea, but there would be no complaints from Alvix. He lay still and Cooper ran the warm damp cloth over his body, wiping up the mess he'd made.

After tossing it back in the direction of the bathroom, Cooper joined Alvix in the bed, where they spooned together, Alvix's back to Cooper's chest. Alvix entwined their hands and rested them on his stomach.

"We should get some sleep. I'm sure Jensen will come and get us before morning," Cooper murmured in his ear.

"You're right."

When Jensen did wake them, their time together would be over, and Alvix didn't really want to think about how long it could be before he saw Cooper again. Closing his eyes, he let Cooper's even breathing soothe him as he imagined what it would feel like to sleep in Cooper's arms every night.

CHAPTER 14

A knock sounded on Alvix's door several hours later. Sitting up, Alvix shoved his hands through his hair and glanced at the clock next to the bed.

"Come in."

Cooper mumbled something Alvix didn't understand as he rolled over and flung his arm over Alvix's lap, burying his face against Alvix's hip.

"Captain Alvix, it's time." Jensen took a few steps inside.

"Time for what?" He ran his hand over Cooper's back, feeling the tension build as Cooper woke.

"You, Corporal Macintosh, and Corporal Gateway must leave within the next ten minutes. The GalMil has demanded General Gateway turn you over within the next twenty-four hours."

Alvix laughed and eased away from Cooper. Climbing out of bed, he mentally ran through a pre-flight checklist.

"I need to take Apple and Pope hostage, disable the tracking device on my ship and fly to Earth. Where I'll begin my new life as some rich man's heir with two personal bodyguards."

"Actually, sir, your tracking unit has already been disabled." Jensen informed him.

Cooper remained silent. Alvix dressed before grabbing his backpack and motioning to Jensen. "Wait outside in the hall for a moment."

She seemed a little taken back by his order, but at Cooper's nod, she left.

Alvix glanced at his lover. Cooper wore his pants and boots, holding his shirt in his hand.

"I guess this is good-bye," Alvix murmured.

Cooper studied him, and Alvix wondered what the man was feeling. With his face all black metal now, Cooper didn't seem as expressive. Alvix watched as Cooper tossed his shirt on the bed and strolled toward him.

Wrapping Alvix in his arms, Cooper held him close. "We'll see each other again. It's only a temporary separation."

Alvix rested his forehead against Cooper's shoulder. He wasn't as optimistic about their chances as Cooper was. Reality had bitten him in the ass too many times before. He didn't want to think about it anymore.

Stepping back, he rose on his toes and pressed a kiss to Cooper's lips. "I have to go."

"I know. The guys will take care of you."

"Of course they will. They respect and fear you too much to do otherwise." He winked before turning and heading out of the room.

"Brat."

Alvix heard Cooper mumble as the man followed behind him. He let a smile cross his lips before sobering and joining Jensen. Buttoning his shirt, Cooper came up beside him and they made their way to the flight area. Apple stood outside Alvix's ship with Callum whispering in his ear. The man's expression didn't change, but Alvix detected he was leaning closer to Callum with each word.

"Where's Pope?" Cooper asked Callum.

"He's already on board, LT. Steele is talking to him. The general's been and gone." Callum saluted before standing at ease.

Apple saluted as well, but stayed silent. Alvix shook his head, wondering if the man was going to start talking soon. If not, Alvix and Pope might run out of things to chat about on the trip to Earth.

"The co-ordinates have been entered into your navigational system, Captain Alvix. We loaded your supplies and informed the landing station on Earth of your arrival. Of course, they know you as Senator Elias Gould's great-nephew, coming to check out your inheritance. The correct papers are on board." Jensen stood next to the ship's door.

"Thank you, Jensen." He held his hand out to the woman. "It was nice meeting you."

"It's been interesting, sir." Jensen shook his hand firmly before strolling away.

Callum nodded toward him, touched Apple on the shoulder, and moved off as well.

Steele left the ship and smiled at Alvix as he went past. "Let these boys take care of you, Alvix. It'll keep them out of trouble and might keep you alive."

"That's all I can ask for, I guess." Alvix chuckled as he gestured for Corporal Macintosh to lead the way into the ship. "You take care of Cooper, Steele. Don't let him do too much."

"We'll do our best. Catch you all on the other side." Steele sketched a wave and joined Callum at the door of the air lock.

"Listen to Apple and Pope. They know what they're doing, and I want you in one piece when I get back to you." Cooper reached out and cupped Alvix's cheek.

"I'll try, but listening isn't really the thing I'm good at." He nuzzled into Cooper's palm for a second. It was all the time he allowed himself to long for things to be different. "You take care of yourself. Don't try any stupid rescues."

Turning, Alvix stalked into his ship, unhappy with how sad he felt. It wasn't right. They hadn't spent that much time together, so he shouldn't be feeling lost already when he just said good-bye to the man. He locked the door and went to his cabin where he dumped his backpack before making his way to the bridge.

Apple sat in the co-pilot seat, staring at the screens. Alvix took his seat with a sigh.

"It sucks."

The softly spoken words caught Alvix off guard. He glanced over at the other man to find Apple looking at him.

"So you do speak?"

Corporal Macintosh shrugged, but didn't seem inclined to talk again.

"It does suck, my friend. I don't think any of us wanted to leave, but we're not being given a choice."

"They'll come get us when things are clear." Apple sounded certain about that.

Alvix grunted, but didn't respond. As far as he was concerned, just because Cooper came back for him once didn't mean the man would do it a second time. They cared for each other in a friendly, fucking kind of way, and if they'd had more time, maybe it would have come to mean more. But they didn't have that time.

He ran through the countdown to engine ignition and when given the all-clear from the flight deck, he took off. Once they broke away from Tative's orbit, he engaged the autopilot to take them to Earth. He wouldn't need to worry about steering until they got clearance to land.

Alvix leaned back in his seat, resting his feet on the console, while staring up at the ceiling. "How are you doing?"

"Seriously?"

Rolling his head to the side, he eyed Apple. "Yeah, seriously."

"I'm fine, considering all the shit we've been through the last several months."

"Right. You don't talk until you're on board a ship with a complete stranger, though you were surrounded by men who care deeply for you." Alvix looked back up at the ceiling.

"Pope isn't up to talking at the moment, and I got the feeling you'd be bouncing off the walls if you didn't have someone to talk to."

"Man, I can talk to myself just as well as chatting with you. Don't put yourself out trying to talk to me." He waved his hand vaguely in Apple's direction. "Do you prefer being called Apple or Macintosh?"

The soldier snorted. "Apple is fine."

"What's your first name?"

"David."

"David? That's your real first name?" Why did that knowledge surprise him?

"Umm...yeah." Apple shifted in his chair. "I'm named after my mom's dad."

"Cool." Alvix grinned. "I don't know why I'm shocked to find out you have a normal name. What's Lieutenant Cooper's first name?"

"I have no idea, Captain."

The bland tone of Apple's voice told Alvix the man lied.

Alvix dropped his feet to the floor and leaned over toward Apple. "Oh, come on. You've been in his unit since you got into boot camp. At some point in time, you had to have heard his name."

Apple eyed him. "I might know what his name is, but I'm not sure he'd want me to blab it all over the place."

"Who the hell am I going to tell?" Alvix gestured around him. "It's only you, Pope, and me on this ship. Anyone we meet on Earth isn't going to give a flying fuck what Cooper's name is."

A chuckle bounced off the bridge, and they both turned to see Pope propped up in the doorway. Apple shot to his feet and raced over to catch the man before he hit the floor.

"What the hell are you doing out of bed?" Apple chastised Pope as he helped him get to a chair.

"I was bored, and you didn't seem to be in a hurry to visit me."

Pope's pale face worried Alvix. He rested his hand on Pope's arm. "Are you okay?"

"I'll be all right. Just haven't moved much lately and this is the most I've done." He looked at the screens. "I'm lonely."

Alvix looked at the other two men. "We are some of the most pathetic men I've seen."

"What do you mean?" Pope shot a look at Apple, who shrugged.

"Never mind." Alvix dug in a drawer under the radar screen console. "Here we go." He held aloft a pack of cards. "Do you guys know how to play poker?"

"Poker?" Apple set up a small table between them.

"It's an old Earth game. We should know it if we're going to be spending any amount of time there."

Alvix broke open the pack and started shuffling the cards. They settled in, laughing and joking as Alvix taught the other two how to play. He decided it was his job to keep their minds off their teammates. Whether they were friends or more, it was still hard being separated from men they'd grown so close to.

CHAPTER 15

Cooper glared at the clerk processing his discharge papers. A low growl rumbled in his chest. Steele, Rivers and Callum surrounded him like they were worried he'd rip the skinny little man's throat out. He waved them away and folded his arms over his chest, tapping his foot impatiently.

"Umm…Captain Cooper, are you sure you don't want to re-up?" The man's voice shook. "Your record is exemplary and you've gotten several good reviews."

"I'm done."

That was all he had to say to any member of the GalMil. After this last mission, where he and his men were used as bait to take over another planet, he'd had enough. It was time to leave, before he ended up flipping out and killing superior officers.

"You as well?" The clerk glanced at Steele, Rivers, and Callum.

His men nodded their heads, not saying a word, their own anger evident in tense muscles and blank faces. The clerk's hand trembled as he pressed his thumb to the pad of their release folders. Cooper did feel bad about frightening the poor guy, but even if they weren't mad, they were still rather imposing. Four tall mostly black metal men staring at him couldn't be good for the man's nerves.

"Here you go."

He barely managed not to rip the folders out of the clerk's hands. "Thanks."

Doing an abrupt about-face, Cooper stalked from the separation office with the others on his heels. He blinked, bringing up the time on his comm unit.

"We have enough time to grab our stuff before the transport General Gateway hired for us is ready to leave," he informed them.

"In a hurry to get out of here, Captain?"

The slimy voice stopped Cooper and his men in their tracks. Whirling around, Cooper clenched his hands to keep from punching the man.

"Yeah. The caliber of soldier has gone downhill since I joined." He eyed Lieutenant Fulcher.

Flucher's thin lips tightened, but the man didn't take the bait. "Could you be on your way to find your missing teammates?"

"They aren't missing," Steele informed the lieutenant.

"Really? Because the GalMil has them listed as AWOL. I'm sure if you were to see them, you would alert the proper authorities."

Callum snorted. "I'm a civilian now, jackass. Two missing soldiers aren't my concern."

Fulcher's pasty skin turned an unattractive shade of pink as the man fought his own anger. Steele, Rivers, and Callum closed ranks around them as Cooper grabbed a handful of Fulcher's shirt and dragged him up on his toes, face-to-face with Cooper.

"Don't be so eager to go looking for Gateway and Macintosh, Fulcher. You might not like what you find if you do." He shook the skinny officer like a terrier with a rat. "We know who you're really looking for and you'll never get your stinking hands on him."

He tossed Fulcher away from him, not monitoring his strength. Fulcher slammed against the metal outside wall of the station. Rivers winced when Fulcher's head bounced off the barrier with a loud thud. They walked away as Fulcher slid to the floor with a whimper.

No one spoke until they were on board the ship General Gateway had provided for them. Callum checked the flight plans filed with the GalMil. Of course, they weren't going to be following them very closely. They had other coordinates, supplied by Jensen, where Alvix, Pope, and Apple had fled to all those months ago.

The silence was broken when they got under way. Cooper sat in the pilot's chair, elbows braced on his knees and hands clasped together. The others found spots around the bridge. Cooper knew their ship would be bug free.

"Where are they?" Callum was the first to voice the question they were all thinking.

"General Gateway lost contact with them two months ago. Pope implied they were being watched." Steele rubbed his palms over his pants.

"They went off the grid." Cooper was certain of that. "Pope and Apple are trained to do that if they think they've been compromised."

"Would Alvix go along with that?" Rivers sounded unsure of what Alvix might do.

Cooper nodded. "To be honest, Alvix never was on the grid. Steele tried to get me information on him and until about five years ago, the man never officially existed. I'd say he knows how to survive without support, considering the first time I ever saw him, he was working as a pickpocket on Raspion."

"You trust him, even though we don't know anything real about him?"

Cooper looked up and met each man's gaze, doing his level best to appear as confident as he felt. "Alvix gave up his freedom and a month of his life for us. I can't—and won't—describe to you the torture he endured while in the possession of the Tongassian king. His actions tell me that he's trustworthy and I need to do everything I can to keep him safe. He wouldn't be in this position if it wasn't for us."

Rivers was the only one who didn't look convinced, but there was no way Cooper could get his friend to believe him. They would have to see it for themselves.

"Flame might be able to show our boys how to survive the old-fashioned way." Steele grinned.

The intercom dinged and Rivers answered it. General Gateway appeared on the screen.

"Gentlemen, I'm sorry to hear you left the military, but I'm glad to see you all are alive."

Callum chuckled. "There's no way anyone was going to take us down, General. The bad guys or the guys we called friends."

Gateway frowned and nodded. "Unfortunately, it's hard to tell them apart."

"We learned that the hard way, sir." Cooper stared down at the floor.

Their last mission was FUBARed from the start. It seemed like someone in command had it in for Cooper and his men. It was no longer a case of an enemy out to get Gateway and his son. Hell, no. Cooper's unit got all the most dangerous missions during the Singer uprising, and often they never had any back-up coming to save their asses. It was pure luck and the grace of God that they all survived with only minor wounds.

It was the very last sojourn into Singer territory that pissed Cooper off to the point he made the decision to quit. The one thing he liked about GalMil was that when a soldier decided to separate from the military, he did so without delay. GalMil probably didn't want any disgruntled soldiers on their hands.

He still had nightmares of watching the two rookie soldiers die under heavy weapons fire, most of which came from behind them and not from the enemy lines. Cooper understood how much someone wanted his men to die, to such an extent that they didn't care that two innocent young men died as well. Cooper and his men had fought their way out, but when they reported it, none of their superior officers believed them. The official report was simply that Cooper's unit was in the wrong place at the wrong time and it was an unfortunate accident.

Guilt ate at him as well because secretly he was glad that Pope and Apple hadn't come with them. He wouldn't have been able to deal with their death by stupidity and jealousy.

"What can you tell us about our guys? Where are they and are they all right?"

He'd deal with his emotions later when he was alone in his cabin.

Gateway gestured off-screen, and Jensen's arm appeared, handing him a sheaf of papers. They waited while he shuffled through them until he found the right one.

"Our last transmission from Corporal Gateway was roughly two months ago. He informed us that their mission had been compromised and they were being watched. They missed their next contact date. We haven't been able to talk to them since then. I sent a man down there, but he can't find them. He's been collecting rumors from the villagers about the men, though."

Gateway's concern showed on his face. Cooper couldn't imagine what it was like to be a father with a missing son. Yet all the men with Pope could handle themselves in case of problems. At least Apple had training, and Cooper had the feeling Alvix wouldn't be a pushover if it came to trouble.

"Do you have the most recent coordinates for them?" Rivers asked.

"Yes. Jensen is sending them to you now. This was the estate Alvix inherited from my friend. Where they've gone since landing, we don't know. No tracking device has been activated, and no one has sighted them."

"Off the grid," Callum muttered.

"Sir, one of our men on site just sent us some information. Villagers spotted three men in the forest. Lights have been seen at the estate house, but no one is brave enough to go up and check on it," Jensen interrupted with excitement in her voice.

"Are they our men?"

Jensen hesitated, and Cooper jumped on it. "What's the problem?"

"Well, he's not sure if it's Corporals Gateway and Macintosh along with Captain Alvix. Two of the men seem to be an odd patchwork of flesh and metal, so it sounds like them. The third man seems to glow at times."

"Glow?"

"What's wrong with Flame?" Steele glanced at him.

"I don't know." Cooper closed his eyes, holding in the urge to order Rivers to turn the engines up and make the ship go faster. "The stress of everything that's happened to him since he met us could be catching up to him. He's never really had to use his power before and his control over it might be weakening."

The general looked puzzled. "Do we know what a fire-eater is or is supposed to be?"

Steele punched some buttons on his wrist harness and all the files he'd gathered on fire-eaters and Alvix popped into the other men's brains, along with showing up on the screen for the general.

"Fire-eaters supposedly come into existence when a star dies. It's never really been proven, or at least not as far as I can tell. I came across several classified files and research to do with fire-eaters. So the story Flame told you about the people he lived with disappearing into labs might be true."

"Jensen, see if you can get those files opened, using my clearance."

"Yes, sir."

"Our friend Captain Alvix didn't come onto the grid until about five years ago. That was when he became a crewmember on a transport ship. Steady promotions and finally he tested for his pilot's license two years ago. He's been clean since then. No brushes with the law or the GalMil. Flies under the radar."

"Until he runs into us and we completely fuck his life up," Cooper murmured, pushing to his feet and walking off the bridge.

He heard low voices talking as he left, but he didn't care if they were talking about him or not. He wasn't a soldier anymore, and while he respected General Gateway, he didn't have to subjugate himself to the man anymore. He didn't have to ask permission for anything.

After returning to his cabin, he lay on his bed, arm flung over his eyes, and waited. It wasn't long before footsteps sounded in the hall outside his room. He didn't react as the door swooshed open and someone stepped in.

"What's wrong?"

Cooper should have known Rivers would be the one sent to check on him. He grunted, not feeling like talking about anything at the moment. Rivers sat on the edge of the bed and rested a hand on Cooper's arm.

"Don't let the guilt eat you alive. Those soldiers knew the cost when they enlisted." Rivers didn't beat around the bush. He got right to the heart of the issue.

Sighing, Cooper peered out from under his arm. "They didn't ask to become a part of our unit and get a big bull's-eye painted on them. The same as Alvix."

Rivers nodded. "Probably not, but it's a risk everyone runs just from living. Being a target isn't simply a military thing, though most military people accept that target willingly. Alvix already had a target on his back because of what he is. Everyone would love to have control of an ability like that."

"He's more than an ability, Rivers. He's a man." Cooper shut his eyes and inhaled deeply. "I know all this. You don't have to explain any of it to me."

"It seems I do...and I'll continue to until you stop beating yourself up over it. None of it was your fault. Seems to me that Alvix and you got to be pretty close while we were on Tative. Shouldn't that be a plus to the whole shitty situation?"

He rolled on his side, meeting Rivers' pure green eyes. "It is a plus, as long as he's still alive when I get to him."

"Have you thought about what we'll do now that we're no longer soldiers?"

"Not really. I was so pissed off that all I could think about was getting away from GalMil as fast as possible." He thought for a second. "Maybe General Gateway knows someone who needs bodyguards."

Rivers grimaced as he stood. "I guess we could become mercs. Good money if you can stay alive long enough to collect it."

"Let's get the rest of our guys before we make plans for our future."

"Got it, sir." Rivers saluted. "We've downloaded the new set of coordinates from Jensen. It'll take us about two weeks to get to Earth.

I'm sure the others can survive that long."

He nodded wearily. Alvix would keep the others safe, even if it meant burning himself out. Flopping over onto his back, he stared up at the ceiling, hoping nightmares wouldn't interrupt his sleep.

CHAPTER 16

"Someone's coming up the drive," Apple whispered as he peeked through the curtains of the parlor.

Alvix pushed away from the corner where he stood. Pope moved with him as they went to stand by Apple at the window. God, he hoped it was some curious child from the village who they could scare away easily with a few noises and some bangs. The ones who were more stubborn, or knew that they were there, tended to need more violent persuasion to leave.

"Is it a kid?"

"I think there are six of them and they move like they've been trained."

He glanced at Pope, and the other man nodded. It was time to head back to the woods. Tapping Apple on the shoulder, he gestured toward the back hallway when the man looked at him.

"I'll bring up the rear." Apple swung his gun up from where it rested against the wall.

"I'd hoped we would get one night in a bed instead of sleeping on the ground." Alvix winced. Shit, he was whining again, and he'd promised himself he would stop complaining about every little thing that went wrong.

Pope patted him on the back when he went past, and Alvix sighed. The general's intentions were good when he sent them here to Earth to hide out, but little did Gateway know that there was someone in his office who'd sold out to the other side. Within a month of landing,

GalMil operatives showed up and it was hiding time for them. Each of them had had their opportunity to take down an agent. Alvix was the only one who hadn't dealt with his kill well.

Of course, Pope and Apple were professional soldiers, so killing for them was just another job. Alvix understood it was kill-or-be-killed, but some small part of him valued the life he took.

Slipping out the back door, he joined Pope at the small barn behind the big house. They housed their horses there for easy escapes. Imagine Alvix's surprise and happiness when they'd arrived at the estate he'd inherited to find those long-legged creatures he'd seen on a postcard once, grazing in his front yard. The horses were tame, and they had used them to get away from the first agents.

He led out his mount and one for Apple, who faced the house and waited for someone to come around the corner of the building.

"We need to head out. Something tells me the GalMil people have gotten impatient and sent out the big guns to take us out." Pope spoke softly as he joined them.

The sound of a door slamming open caught their ears and they mounted, knowing it was only a matter of time before someone thought to check the back yard. They headed into the thick growth of trees, following a deer trail that wound its way through the forest to the river. They never went that far, but the deer used the trail every night, so their hoof prints erased the horses' tracks.

As they slipped into the shadow-darkened forest, Alvix heard a shout before a loud report. Something slammed into his back and he bit through his lip to keep from crying out. Pope dropped back, grabbed the reins of his horse and started leading him down another path. Apple took the point, checking behind them once in a while.

Night fell as they made their way to one of their hiding spots. Alvix weaved in the saddle, drained from pain and loss of blood. Not wanting to leave a blood trail, they'd taken the time to bandage the wound.

"The bastards shot me," he muttered as Pope helped him dismount.

"It would seem like it." Apple pushed aside the brush they used to cover the cave opening, so Pope and Alvix could make their way in. "I'll go hide our trail as best I can, though if they're military, they'll know what to look for."

"At the moment, I don't give a flying fuck who they are. If they get close, I'll fry their asses."

Pope and Apple exchanged glances. Alvix could see the worry in their eyes and he patted Apple's shoulder as they passed.

"Don't worry. I'm not going crazy. I'm in pain and it makes me cranky." He inhaled sharply as Pope lowered him to the ground. "I'm not going to burn you either."

"That's good to know." Pope waved a hand at Apple. "Go and get that taken care of. We'll get the fire going, and I'll deal with Alvix's wound."

After Apple left, Alvix gritted his teeth as Pope peeled the bandage away from the back of his shoulder. He winced at each poke of Pope's fingers.

"How's it look?"

"Well, the bleeding has stopped for the moment, but the bullet's still in there."

"You mean they shot me with a real bullet? Not a laser weapon or something like that?" He leaned forward, resting his forehead on his drawn-up knees.

Pope chuckled softly. "Probably didn't want to take draw attention to themselves. There aren't a lot of modern military grade weapons on Earth anymore. Just the primitive guns they had before the mass exodus."

"Shit. That really sucks."

"It gets better. The bullet didn't go all the way through. I'm going to have to dig it out."

Shooting a glance over his shoulder, he met Pope's unhappy gaze. "Have you ever done anything like that before?"

"No." Pope shook his head. "The battles I've been in, all sides were equipped with the newest weapons. No real bullets fired."

"Tell me again why we came to this fucking backward planet?"

"At the moment, I can't begin to figure out why it sounded like a good idea at the time."

Alvix sighed and made the decision. Not that he had any choice. It was dig the bullet out or let the wound get infected, then his arm would rot off. "Let's do it."

"I'll have to wait until Apple gets back," Pope informed Alvix. "I can't do it on my own."

The young soldier was silent for a minute or two. Alvix looked back at him and caught the worried look on Pope's face.

"What's up?"

Pope met his gaze and smiled wanly. "Will the guys come back for us?"

Not stopping the rather hysterical laughter bursting from his lips,

Alvix shook his head in disbelief. "Your friends mounted an almost-certain-to-fail rescue mission to retrieve three of you. Do you seriously think they wouldn't come here? Earth is child's play compared to Tongass, even if there are GalMil soldiers wandering around the stupid planet."

"Thanks." Pope squeezed Alvix's uninjured shoulder quickly.

He waved away the soldier's words and closed his eyes, trying to dampen the pain. He didn't know if his words really helped or not, but he figured it didn't matter if he believed them himself. Keeping Pope and Apple's morale up was the most important thing to Alvix, who was used to being left behind. But those two men had never been abandoned in their lives.

Distant sounds of firearms caught their attention. Pope shot him a quick look before heading toward the entrance of the cave, taking up a defensive position.

"That wasn't close. I think we're still okay."

Apple dove into the cave, chest heaving and sweat on his brow.

"Were they shooting at you?" Pope managed to snag a bottle of water from one of their packs and tossed it to Apple.

Apple shook his head. "No. They're fighting someone else. Don't know who. I didn't stick around to find out."

"Good idea. We'll hang tight here for a while."

"Catch your breath because you're going to have to help me operate on Alvix. I have to get the bullet out of his shoulder."

"Seriously?" Apple grimaced as he met Alvix's gaze. "That sucks, man."

"You're telling me." Alvix gestured toward the back of the cave. "Get the fire set up. I'll start it when you're done."

Pope started getting the few medical supplies they had out while Apple stacked firewood. When Apple finished, Alvix held out his hand and concentrated. The pain made it more difficult to focus, but he corralled his power and, with a soft pop, the wood burst into flames.

His shoulders slumped and his head dropped as his strength left him. Apple caught him and helped move him closer to the fire.

"We could've started it the old-fashioned way," Apple grumbled.

"Why take the time when I can do it in seconds?" Alvix stroked his fingers over Apple's cheek. "I'll be okay. Pope will get the bullet out, and we'll hang on until the rest arrive to get us."

Lying on his side, facing the fire, Alvix closed his eyes and listened to Pope and Apple as they moved around the cave.

"Can you do this?" Apple's question was low, but Alvix could still hear it.

"In theory. It's not like we ever needed any of that field medic training they gave us in the academy, but I don't have a choice. We can't take him to a hospital because whoever's looking for us would be sure to find us there."

"I know, but still, this is going to hurt. We don't have anything to dull the pain."

Pope sighed. "I know, Apple, but it's either take it out, or leave it in and let the wound fester. Either way, it's going to be a bitch and very painful."

Apple's frustration was clear in his sigh. "I wish they'd get here already. It's been over six months and we've been on the run for two. What's taking them so long?"

"They were sent on a mission. You know that we've never known how long one might take. The lieutenant and the others will get here as soon as they can. We just have to stay free until they do."

"Do you really believe they're coming for us? I mean, neither of us will be viable fighting material again. Why would the team come rescue us?"

"We're more than fighting machines to Steele, Callum, and the others. We're their family. Bonds exist among all of us that can never be broken." Pope's voice dropped lower. "Besides, LT has the hots for Flame over there."

Alvix's cheeks warmed, and it wasn't because of the fire.

Apple laughed. "Well, Steele's pretty attached to you as well, so I'm sure he'll be coming back for your ass."

"What about you, Callum, and Rivers? Did you ever figure out what's going on with the three of you?" Pope swore softly. "We'll need to rip up a blanket or two. There aren't enough bandages."

Alvix heard noises he assumed was Apple digging through their supplies. A violent ripping sound startled him, and he jumped, biting back a cry as pain shot through his body.

"Things were fine with us before we got captured by the Tongassians. Now they won't touch me. It's like I'm tainted or poisoned somehow."

Alvix couldn't keep eavesdropping like that. He rolled slowly onto his back, glad for the thick bandage Pope had stuck on before they laid him down. Apple and Pope glanced over at him. After waving them over, he took their hands in his.

"They're afraid of hurting you. More than likely, they're afraid anything they do to you might trigger a flashback of what happened to you on that planet."

"How do you know that?" Apple eyed him suspiciously. "Did they talk to you?"

Shaking his head, he grinned. "No. It's the same way Cooper felt before I convinced him what he did to me was nothing like what the king did. I can tell the difference. I have issues from that time, but I'm not letting that bastard have any more control of me."

He squeezed Apple's hands. "You just have to convince them that you won't break. That their touch will help you heal from the trauma."

Apple seemed to be thinking about Alvix's advice as he went back to getting the things ready for bullet removal. Pope stayed next to Alvix.

"Both Callum and Rivers?" Alvix asked quietly, not wanting Apple to hear.

Pope nodded. "The planet Apple's from doesn't look down on male pairing. They actually encourage it, along with multiple partners."

"Why can't all planets be as enlightened as his?"

"Don't know."

He glanced up at Pope. Those dark brown eyes flecked with gold weren't staring at Apple. They gazed at the fire with a pensive feel.

"How about you and Steele? Are you still good?"

"Well, we were solid when we split up six months ago, but who knows now?"

Alvix closed his eyes against the sudden pain. He clenched his jaw and forced the words out. "I'm sure it'll be fine. Might be a few awkward moments when you first see each other, but it'll work out."

Pope held his hand and didn't react as Alvix's grip got stronger. "I bet you didn't know you'd have to be a relationship counselor when you took up with us."

"Gives me something to take my mind off my own problems." He peered through his eyelashes at Pope.

"You have nothing to worry about. The LT must really like you because I've never seen him as worked up as he was when we left you behind on Tongass. I thought Rivers was going to have to knock him out and strap him in. He was tenacious and determined that we were going back for you, no matter what the GalMil had to say about it. My father had to make up some mission so we got permission to go off the reservation and get you."

Those words eased Alvix a little. He still wasn't sure if Cooper would want to pursue a relationship once all the stress and excitement ended, but he couldn't help hoping he would.

CHAPTER 17

"Dead?"

"As a doornail." Rivers straightened from where he crouched next to the fallen soldier. "He's GalMil; even got the serial number brand on his neck."

They imprinted all GalMil soldiers with a serial number and tracking brand when they entered boot camp. It was the easiest way for the military to keep track of them. Cooper rubbed the back of his neck where his brand used to be. The metal on his body covered the brand and made it impossible for the GalMil to know where he was. That was the way he liked it.

"Good." Turning, he searched for Steele. "Got any tracks yet?"

"There's a mixture of tracks. I've downloaded information, so I can figure out what kind of animals made each set." Steele scanned the dirt in front of him.

"Hey, Coop," Callum called from the edge of the trail where he stood, studying a branch higher up a tree trunk.

"What have you got?" He strolled over.

Callum plucked a leaf from the branch and held it out to Cooper. "Blood."

"Shit. That means one of them was shot." He snarled, fighting the need to go back and kick the dead men.

"And with real bullets." Joining them, Rivers gestured to the high-powered rifle one of the soldiers had been carrying when they ambushed them.

Cooper shook his head. "This isn't good. They aren't equipped to operate on each other. We need to find them and get them on the ship before anything else happens to them. Something seems to be blocking our internal link."

"Got them." Steele waved a hand to get their attention. "There are horse tracks mixed in with deer. They split off from the main trail right here."

Steele pointed to a faint path splitting off from the wider track.

"We'll follow this, but keep your eyes open. They could've left the path at any point or abandoned the horses and continued on foot. Also, shout out if you see any more drops of blood."

He waved to the others to head out while he stood for a moment, staring at the bloody leaf in his hand. His heart skipped a beat and his mouth went dry. Who had been shot and how bad was it? Would they be in time? Was it going to be another death because of jealousy?

Rivers' hand appeared in his line of sight and grabbed the leaf away from him. "Stop it," his friend commanded. "You only get to freak out if one of them is actually dead. Anyway, it's not your fault this time."

"Not my fault? How can you say that?"

"Because while these guys were sent by probably the same person who'd love to see all of us dead, they were after Flame, not our boys."

"He's one of us now," Cooper pointed out, following behind Rivers as his friend led the way to catch up with the others.

"Yeah, he is, but you need to stop taking all this shit on your shoulders, Coop. None of this is your fault. It's no one's fault except the bastard who decided they wanted to get rid of us." Rivers tilted his head and thought for a moment. "And the scientists who think experimenting on Flame will reveal all his secrets."

Cooper wasn't sure he agreed with his friend, but it was better not to argue any more. They stalked silently through the forest, eyes trained to pick out discrepancies in the leaf cover and among the branches closest to the trail. He nodded when Steele pointed out more blood wetting the dirt on the side of the path.

Callum, who had the point, stopped and held up his hand, signaling for everyone to halt. He pointed to his nose and gestured to the right where a pile of brush sat. Cooper sniffed softly and noticed the burnt scent of fire. Someone was burning wood someplace close.

He nodded, and Callum crept closer to the brush pile. As the others began to circle around, a pain-filled scream rocketed through the forest and it came from behind the pile. Cooper completely forgot about rules and all that shit. He yanked the barrier out of the way and dashed into the cave behind it.

Apple shot to his feet, handgun raised and pointed at Cooper. Alvix lay face down next to a fire with Pope hunched over him.

"Don't shoot, Apple. It's us." Cooper held his hands up.

"Apple, get your ass over here and hold Flame down. He's moving too much. I can't get a hold of the bullet."

Both Apple and Cooper dropped to their knees next to the prone Alvix. Cooper ran his hand down Alvix's arm to clasp his hand in his. Apple braced both hands on Alvix's back, keeping the man from moving. Rivers, Callum, and Steele stood at the entrance of the cave to stay out of the way.

"Cooper, is that you?"

Alvix's voice was harsh, and in the flickering flames of the fire, Cooper spotted blood on Alvix's bottom lip. He'd been biting it to keep from shouting.

"Yeah, we're here now. You can scream all you want, baby. The guys will keep the enemy away."

He glanced up to see Pope and Apple staring at him. He quirked the corner of his mouth to encourage them.

"We need to get this done, so we can take all of you back to the house."

"We can't go back there," Apple said. "They know where we are."

Rivers came over and caressed the top of Apple's head. "You've got back-up now, Apple. It's time to make our stand."

Cooper again had the weirdest feeling he was missing something. Maybe once all of it got straightened out, he'd sit with his men and asking them what the hell was going on among all of them.

"Steele," Pope called, "you've got steadier hands than I do. Come and see if you can get this bullet out of there."

Steele shoved his gun at Callum and dropped next to Pope. Cooper watched as Pope handed him the large forceps he'd been using. A low moan filled the hot air, and Cooper wasn't sure if it came from him or Alvix as the instrument slid into the wound. Alvix's hand tightened to the point of almost crushing Cooper's hand. He was glad he was more metal than flesh because even so he'd probably be bruised the next day.

"Just a little farther." Steele grunted, baring his teeth as he dug deeper into Alvix's flesh.

Cooper leaned down and pressed his mouth to Alvix's ear. "I'm here. Listen to my voice. I'll get you through this."

He kept talking, babbling about whatever he could think of. He didn't know if it made any difference or not, but he was powerless to do anything else. At one point, Alvix moaned and passed out.

"Thank God," Pope murmured. "He's tougher than I give him credit for. I thought he'd pass out a while ago."

"Got it." Steele tugged the forceps out and held up the bullet. "Stitch it up and we'll get him ready to go back to the house."

Apple and Pope did the closing and bandaging while the others gathered up the rest of the supplies.

"Where are the horses?" Rivers asked Apple.

"They're in another cave about four klicks from here."

"Go with him to get them, Rivers." Cooper caught the looks among Rivers, Callum, and Apple. "Callum, go with them."

After the trio disappeared outside, Pope chuckled. "That might not be a good idea, LT."

"I'm no longer in the military. Actually, none of us is. The GalMil consider you and Apple AWOL, but I think that's because someone is doing their damnedest to screw this unit. You can call me Cooper."

"Right, sir. You know, Flame asked Apple what your first name was."

"Did he tell him?" Not that he really cared if Alvix knew his name or not.

Pope shook his head. "Of course not. He wouldn't talk out of turn."

"When the hell did he start talking again?" Cooper scratched his chin. "Hell, I don't think I remember Rivers' first name."

"Jackson." Pope looked up from finishing Alvix's bandage and seemed to ignore Cooper's question. "You want to carry Alvix out? He probably won't wake up until we're at the house."

"Why wasn't it a good idea to send those three for the horses?" He swept Alvix into his arms and headed toward the outside.

Steele shoved the brush aside to let Cooper out. Pope and Steele brought the packs of supplies out to where Cooper stood.

"Because Apple, Rivers, and Callum are a threesome. I'm hoping the enforced separation allowed them to work through some issues they were having." Pope dropped the bags on the ground and leaned on a tree.

After sitting, Cooper cradled Alvix in his lap, while he tried to wrap his mind around the fact three of his men were sleeping together. Steele stood close to Pope, their shoulders brushing. Okay, so it looked like all of his men were sleeping with each other.

"How did I miss it?" he muttered.

Before Steele or Pope could reply, Alvix jerked awake. Cooper kept his hands away from Alvix's shoulder, but held him tight.

"It's all right, Alvix."

"Fuck. I hurt everywhere." Alvix reached up and stroked his fingers down Cooper's nose. "Did they get the bullet out?"

"Steele managed to get it out. The others are getting the horses." He kissed Alvix's fingers as they passed over his lips.

Alvix looked around and spotted Steele and Pope nearby. "Maybe we should get started back toward the house. It might take the others a little while to get back with the horses."

Cooper burst out laughing, along with the other two men. Alvix shot looks at all of them with a puzzled frown on his face.

"Pope just said sort of the same thing. Don't worry. I'm pretty sure they'll do their job and wait to celebrate their reunion later."

"You know we *can* control ourselves." Rivers stepped from the forest to their left, leading one of the horses. Callum and Apple were right behind him.

"Thank God for that. I didn't relish carrying Alvix's gimpy ass all the way back to the house." Cooper grinned at Alvix's frown.

They loaded the packs on two of the horses and Cooper helped Alvix mount the other. He walked beside the animal, resting his hand on its neck or Alvix's thigh. Whenever Alvix weaved slightly, Cooper would brace him to insure he didn't fall off. Alvix averted his gaze when they passed the dead GalMil soldiers.

"We heard one of the strangers glowed."

Apple's harsh laugh rang through the woods. "Flame glowed after he torched one of the guys hunting us. He tends to be brighter after starting a fire or healing one of us."

"When did you start talking again? Pope never did answer that question."

Shrugging, Apple glanced at Pope and Alvix. "We had just taken off to come here. It made sense to talk. I figured Pope wouldn't really be up to conversation, and Flame isn't the type of guy to handle silence well."

"Why didn't you talk sooner?"

"Didn't have anything important to say, and I was working things out in my head." Apple glanced out into the shadowed forest. "I still have moments when I'm not right in my mind."

Callum reached out and stroked his hand over Apple's shoulder.

112

"We all have times like that, especially after this past year."

"Hell, I have moments like that after decades of living. You aren't any different from the rest of us." Alvix closed his eyes for a second, breathing deeply.

Cooper eyed him, not liking the paleness of Alvix's skin or the sweat beading on his forehead. "How much longer, Pope?"

Pope threw a glance over his shoulder at Alvix slumped on the horse. "Not much farther, sir. When we reach the tree line, Steele and I will go and check the house. Make sure no one's shown up while we were gone."

"Good idea." He wasn't going to argue about who was in charge. Since they were no longer in the military, he didn't outrank any of the guys, so they could make their own decisions.

Being trained military men, they knew what they had to do to keep themselves and others safe. Maybe security jobs would be a way for them to make money after they got out of this situation alive. He'd talk it over with them later.

Steele raised a hand, bringing the group to a stop right before they broke cover. After handing their rifles to Callum and Rivers, Pope and Steele slipped away into the twilight, heading for the house to clean it out in case anyone was there to ambush them.

While they waited, Cooper helped Alvix off the horse and allowed the man to lean on him. He slipped his arm around Alvix's waist, trying not to think about how skinny the man had become. He nuzzled his face into Alvix's hair and breathed in the salty scent of Alvix's sweat. Alvix slid his arms around Cooper's neck, crushed their lips together, and Cooper came home.

Their mouths fed off each other. Their tongues stroked and teased. Cooper ran his hands down to cup Alvix's ass, rocking their groins together.

Coughing broke them apart, and Alvix buried his face against Cooper's chest as Cooper looked up to see his men staring at them. Smirks graced their faces, and he smiled ruefully.

"And you were worried we couldn't keep our hands off Apple," Rivers joked.

"Sorry," Alvix mumbled.

"No worries." Callum patted Alvix's uninjured shoulder.

"The house is clear. We can move."

Pope returned and gestured for them to follow him. Without listening to Alvix's protests, Cooper swept the man up in his arms and carried him to the house. Apple led him upstairs to one of the bedrooms. He laid Alvix down and, almost instantly, Alvix fell asleep.

"We'll let him rest."

They returned downstairs to find the others putting the supplies away in the kitchen and other rooms. He gathered them up with a glance and they went to the living room where they found spots to sit.

CHAPTER 18

Pope and Steele sat close together on the loveseat while Apple, Callum, and Rivers took over the couch. Cooper remained standing, his hands clasped behind his back.

"We have a problem."

"Oh, really? I thought we were all safe and sound here without any worries at all."

Apple's smart-ass comment earned him some dirty looks.

"I think you've been hanging around Alvix too long." Cooper paced in front of them.

"That's entirely possible." Apple grunted as Callum elbowed him. "What?"

"Shut up and let the captain talk," Rivers admonished Apple.

Holding up his hand, Cooper stopped them. "I'm not a captain anymore. None of us is a soldier. Pope, you'll want to talk to your father. Maybe he can get the stupid AWOL charges dropped for you and Apple. After that, you'll both have to decide whether to stay in the military or separate like the rest of us did."

Pope studied all of them. "So you really did leave the service. Why?"

"Couldn't take the bullshit anymore." Steele shook his head. "Everywhere we turned on the last mission, someone was shooting at us, and it wasn't just the enemy."

"Someone is out to get us. Maybe if we aren't the elite unit in the GalMil, they'll leave us alone." Cooper joined in the laughter as the others showed their disbelief in that comment. "I know. It's too much to hope for, but you know what? This house will serve us as a base camp. The general will supply us with any weapons we need or want. If Alvix throws in with us, we'll have the money to buy food and make this place viable."

"What can we do to bring in money? We can't live off Flame's inheritance." Callum looked around.

The others nodded, and Cooper chuckled. "Glad to know you all feel that way. I'm going to suggest we discuss our future later when we aren't being hunted by GalMil soldiers." Cooper looked at Pope. "Go contact your father. Let him know you're okay and that we got here all right. We'll be sending him a list of supplies and things."

Pope nodded and stood. Cooper caught his arm before he left the room. "I'm sure the general knows this, but tell him to be very careful who he tells about us."

"I will."

"Is Jensen trustworthy?" He hated even thinking she might be one of the people trying to get rid of them, but if he was to keep his men alive, he wouldn't trust the general when it came down to it.

"She better be or it'll kill my father. They've been sleeping together since she joined his office." Pope grinned at Cooper's surprised expression. "He doesn't know I know, but I figure what the hell. He's been lonely since my mother died, and Jensen seems good for him. I'm not going to hassle him about it."

"Shit, he better hope no one gets wind of that or his career is dead. She's a lower-ranking officer and a woman. Not good for their careers."

"Maybe not, but it's good for their lives, and that's all that's important as far as I'm concerned. It's none of my business anyway. They're adults."

Cooper waved Pope on before turning to look at the others. "Why don't the rest of you set up a perimeter and an early warning system, in case they send anyone else after us?"

Steele jumped to his feet. "Sir, yes, sir."

He flipped his friends off as they left the room, joking and wrestling with each other. In the silence that fell after they were gone, Cooper looked around him. Shit, he'd never seen any room that looked like this one. Rich mahogany-colored wood covered the floors, and he assumed it was real wood, not synthetic crap. Everything in here spoke of money, old money. The kind of money that was around when Earth ruled the universe.

Of course, Earth wasn't anything more than a resort for obscenely rich families wanting to connect with their ancient past now. The people who lived on the planet and didn't just visit were poor. They farmed or found work at the houses of the off-planet visitors.

"Hey, Apple," he yelled.

"Yeah?"

"Were there servants here when you arrived?"

Apple stuck his head around the wall and nodded. "Sure, but the minute the GalMil showed up and started shooting at us, they bailed."

"Can't say I blame them. This isn't their fight." He rubbed his chin while he thought. "I wonder if we could get some of them to come back. Now that we're here, things should be a little safer. We'll need someone to take care of Alvix."

A small wrinkle appeared between Apple's brows as the man thought. "I could probably go and find out. Maybe offer them more than they were making when the old bastard owned the place."

"Go in the morning and take Callum with you. If anyone can charm someone, it'd be that man." Cooper flicked through the different time codes in his inter-face and found the Earth one. "It's almost eleven. We've been on the move since early this morning. Figure out the watch. I'm going to crash for a while and have whoever wake me up for the last watch."

"Go to bed, Coop. We've got things under control. If we need you, we know where to find you." Apple slapped him on the back as he went by.

Cooper climbed up the stairs and went to Alvix's room. He probably shouldn't share the man's bed. He'd have to make sure not to hit Alvix's wounded shoulder. Stripping in the dark room, he thought about all those nights during his mission in the Singer Galaxy when he would remember what it felt like to share a bed with someone, to listen to him breathe, to feel his warmth in his arms. Each time he imagined the man he held it would be Alvix's face he saw.

After slipping under the blankets, he carefully wrapped Alvix in his embrace and rested his cheek on Alvix's head, counting the number of heartbeats he felt, reassuring himself that Alvix was alive.

"Everything secure, Cooper?" Alvix's question was low as Alvix ran his hand down Cooper's back.

"For now. We'll regroup tomorrow and figure out who we're looking for."

"They want me. Why not just give me up? Maybe they'll leave you alone if they have me."

He stiffened at Alvix's suggestion. Pushing Alvix onto his back, Cooper braced himself with his hands on either side of Alvix's head and glared down at the man.

"You already sacrificed yourself once for us. I'm not going to allow you to do it again. Not when I have the means to keep us all safe." Cooper shook his head. "Don't even think about walking out of here without me."

"Why does it matter?" Alvix's confusion was evident in his question. "I don't see why you should care that much for me."

"Because I love you, damn it."

*　　*　　*

Alvix's heart stopped at Cooper's words. There was no way he heard that right. "You don't mean that."

"I don't? Well, thank you very much for telling me what I mean and don't mean." Cooper growled.

"Honest, why would you love me?" He smiled hesitantly. "The sex was awesome. Would be again, I'm sure, if I was up to having it. Not sure great sex equates to love."

He stopped talking as Cooper pressed his fingers to his lips.

"I will admit I've had great sex before you and I hooked up, but I've never thought about them afterward. None of them ever affected how I did my job." Cooper winked at him with a grin. "You did and do."

Puzzled, Alvix opened his lips and licked Cooper's fingers while he thought about what Cooper had said. His lover shuddered as he sucked those thick, rough digits into his mouth.

"Fuck. I told myself we wouldn't do anything because your shoulder needs to heal."

Cooper rubbed his erection against Alvix's thigh. With a sigh, he let Cooper's fingers slide from his mouth.

"I know, and you're right. Even now there's this underlying ache I can't forget about." He rested Cooper's hand on his chest.

"Are you going to say anything about the fact I told you I loved you or are you just going to ignore it?"

He thought about it, and Cooper frowned.

"I have to be honest and say I want to ignore it because I don't believe you. I mean, really, you're in love with me? How can that be when we hardly know each other? Trust me, if you spent any time with me, you'd come to hate my little quirks and habits. I'm not an easy person to live with. No one's wanted to stay with me at any point in my life."

Snapping his mouth shut, he stopped the babble pouring out. Okay, so Cooper didn't need to know all of his insecurities and shit. Of course, maybe he should find out, simply because then Cooper might walk away from him and he'd be alone like usual.

"And you haven't spent any true time with me. You could end up hating me or my personality. I know great sex doesn't mean a good relationship outside of bed." Cooper cupped Alvix's face in his hand. "I'd like to try and see what we can make after this whole fucked-up situation is taken care of."

Cooper rolled over on his back, dragging Alvix with him. Alvix wiggled around, settling into the curve of Cooper's arm and resting his head on Cooper's shoulder. He flung his arm over Cooper's stomach and relaxed as the pain eased from the stitches. He felt Cooper's breath flutter his hair as they fell asleep.

CHAPTER 19

The sound of the door opening woke Alvix and he sat up as Rivers took a step into the room.

"What's wrong, Rivers?" He shook Cooper gently.

"Nothing's wrong. It's Coop's turn to keep guard." Rivers didn't move any closer.

Cooper came awake and sat up, swinging his legs over the edge. "I'll be right out, Rivers. Thanks."

"No problem." Rivers shut the door behind him.

Alvix leaned back against the headboard while Cooper stood. He watched Cooper dress.

"Why are you guys keeping watch?"

Sitting, Cooper glanced over his shoulder before putting his boots on. "We don't know for sure how many GalMil soldiers were sent. There might be more out there or more could have arrived, plus it's always good practice to keep an eye out. The villagers might not be hostile, but we can't guarantee they won't turn on us."

Alvix nodded. It made sense, even though Alvix had never had to worry about that, except for Weldon.

"I wonder what happened to Weldon," he muttered aloud.

Cooper's grin was sort of smug. "I hear he ran afoul of some GalMil regulations and ended up on a penal planet. We'll see how long he lasts there."

"Who do I thank for that?" He smiled, glad to hear he wouldn't have to worry about Weldon ever again. He gasped as Cooper swooped in and kissed him hard.

As he recovered from that, Cooper walked out, saying, "You have the general to thank for that. I didn't have anything to do with it."

It took a few minutes, but Alvix finally cleared his mind and climbed out of bed. He scrounged up some clothes and tugged them on, moving carefully so he didn't rip open his injury.

Wandering down, he nodded at Pope and Steele as they passed him on the stairs. Rivers was bringing Cooper up to speed on what happened while they slept when Alvix walked into the kitchen.

"It looks like things are quiet. Pope and Steele are heading up to grab some rest. Callum and Apple took the first shift. The general wants to talk to you later today." Rivers glanced over at Alvix and nodded. "The chatter on the lines is that the fire-eater has been found. I'm thinking we might be having visitors and not just GalMil people either."

"Mercs and bounty hunters." Alvix nodded. "I'm sure whoever wants me will team up with whoever wants you and come hunting both of us."

"That's what I'd do if it was me wanting you," Cooper mumbled, pouring a cup of java for himself.

"Pour me one of those." Alvix nodded at the java pot. "You didn't need any help getting me. Just fixed my ship and saved me from Weldon. My own personal knight in shining armor."

Cooper looked down at his own hand. "Quite literally in armor."

Alvix glanced at Rivers who nodded.

"I'll see you later. I'm heading up to get some sleep."

"Good night, Rivers." Alvix smiled.

Cooper just grunted, but didn't look up from where he stood, staring down at his hands. Alvix pushed their cups toward the middle of the counter, lifted Cooper's hands, and slipped in front of him to lean his ass against the edge. Instead of saying anything, Alvix slipped his arm around Cooper's neck, savoring the coolness of the man's metal skin.

He'd been using his fire so much lately, it seemed he was running a permanent fever. Only Cooper could ease the heat rising in him. Alvix rested his forehead against Cooper's chest, closed his eyes and breathed in the unique scent of metal and male.

"There are times when I think the scientists who created the nano-mites were geniuses."

Alvix chuckled and agreed. "You're right. You are more like a robot than a human, but at least, they didn't figure out how to take away your emotions."

"That's probably next. They want to create totally unfeeling soldiers who will kill without question and do anything they want them to do." Cooper frowned down at Alvix.

"Every military in the history of the universe has tried to remove the human element from their fighters and as technology advances, they'll be able to do it. I've met true cyborgs and those creatures are creepy."

He ran a finger over Cooper's chin, down his throat to the middle of his chest where Alvix pressed the palm of his hand against it. Cooper's heart beat reassuringly under his touch.

"You're still very human and that must frustrate the people who made you. They weren't expecting you and your men to decide working for them wasn't all it was meant to be."

"I have a confession to make. If it wasn't for the Tongassian debacle and meeting you, I'd probably still be in the military and doing what I was told."

Knocking at the back door broke them apart. Cooper turned, drawing the gun at his hip.

"Go get the others," he whispered, and Alvix had no choice but to obey. It wasn't like he could fight.

The kitchen plunged into darkness as he made his way back upstairs to the bedrooms. He knocked on the ones he knew Apple and Pope had used before they went to ground. Steele opened one and Callum opened the other.

"What is it, Flame?"

He heard rustling in both rooms as the others got dressed.

"Someone's here. They knocked on the back door. Cooper sent me to get you."

Rivers and Apple appeared behind Callum, while Pope left the room with Steele. The soldiers trooped down stairs, keeping Alvix inside their protective circle. He hid his smile at the way they unconsciously kept him safe, even though he didn't necessarily need their protection.

"It's all right, though you all need to be in on this discussion." Cooper stepped from the kitchen with Jensen following him.

"Jensen." Pope rushed down the rest of the stairs to where his father's lover stood. "Where's Father?"

"They came at us in the middle of the night. I guess they thought our defenses lower during that time, but they don't know the general very well. He had enough warning to stuff me on a transport ship and program it to come here." Tears filled Jensen's eyes. "I didn't want to leave him."

Pope embraced her tight against him. "I know you didn't, but he's your commanding officer. You had to do what he wanted you to do. How long ago was this?"

Jensen relaxed in Pope's arms for a few minutes, and no one pushed her to answer. Alvix skirted the group and went into the kitchen. Things were coming to a head, now that the GalMil had taken the supreme general into custody. It wouldn't be long before the entire resources of the military came to bear on them. Definitely needed a full breakfast and java for this discussion.

He had food cooking on the stove when Callum entered the room.

"What are you doing?"

"Tell everyone to gather in the dining room. Breakfast is ready and it'll be better to make plans on a full stomach." Alvix started plating the food and handed a platter full of bacon to Callum.

"Yes, sir," Callum quipped before exiting the room.

Alvix rolled his eyes and finished gathering the rest of the food.

"Where are the plates?" Steele strolled in.

"Over there." Alvix nodded toward the set of cupboards over by the sink.

Steele grabbed enough plates and silverware for everyone, while Callum returned for the java and mugs. No one spoke until after breakfast was devoured and the java refilled. Cooper pushed his empty plate away and cleared his throat, drawing everyone's attention.

"Okay. Jensen tells me that we have maybe a twenty-four hour window to get ready for them coming after us."

"Fuck." Rivers growled as he shoved his plate away as well.

"Why did they take the general?" Alvix leaned forward to rest his elbows on the table.

"They knew he'd let you go. They probably never believed his story that you overpowered both Pope and Apple, forcing them to take you to your ship and keeping them hostage, but they had no proof. Without proof, you can't accuse a supreme general of lying." Jensen fiddled with her fork. "There was no time to search out the informant in our midst. Not that it matters anymore. The base on Tative is gone. The GalMil destroyed it before they left."

"It can always be rebuilt." Cooper rubbed his chin while he thought. "We know the general has powerful friends, so at the moment, we'll have to hope they'll be able to get him out."

Alvix knew not doing anything for the general didn't sit well with Pope or the other men, but Cooper was right. There was no way their small group could execute a successful rescue, not even with Alvix giving himself up to their pursuers. The general was sequestered at GalMil headquarters, and no one broke in or out of there.

"I brought you supplies—weapons, ammo, and food. Radios for communication and medical supplies." She stood. "I have to head out now. It's time for me to start recruiting all those powerful contacts."

"Do you have people with you?" Pope and Steele stood.

"Yes, but I left them at the ship."

"Pope, you and Steele go back to the ship with Jensen. Get it unloaded and get your asses back here as soon as you can."

"Yes, sir." Pope and Steele nodded as they followed Jensen out of the house.

"Someone should warn the villagers that there might be hostiles arriving soon." Cooper looked at Apple and Callum. "The two of you go down there and let them know. If they want weapons, we'll give them to them."

"The GalMil doesn't want the natives armed," Rivers reminded Cooper.

"Fuck the GalMil. We know why they don't want any of the natives armed. They might end up defending their planet like the Tongassians did." Cooper stood and met Rivers' gaze. "I realize we're taking a chance that they'll turn on us, but I refuse to leave them helpless when they'll be caught in the cross-fire because of us."

"Yes, sir." Callum and Apple grabbed up their weapons and headed out to the village just a few klicks down the road.

"What are we doing?" Alvix looked between Rivers and Cooper.

"What do you mean?" Rivers gestured for them to come with him.

"Why are you getting ready to fight these people? It doesn't make any sense. Turn me over to them. Now you're no longer a part of the military, maybe they'd let you walk away."

"We've already discussed this. I'm not turning you over to them. Not to let them experiment on you. What about all those people you saw disappear into the labs and never come out? Do you want to be a lab rat the rest of your life?" Cooper glared at him.

Alvix chuckled and patted Cooper on the shoulder. "Of course I don't, but give me some credit. I'm capable of taking care of myself even against soldiers of GalMil."

"Why would you risk it when you have us to keep you safe?"

"You're right. I should just let you do what you do best." He turned and picked up some of the plates on the table.

"What are you doing?" Cooper and Rivers stopped in the doorway.

"I'm cleaning up. You don't need me around while you do whatever you do best."

Rivers pursed his lips and headed out, obviously not wanting to get involved with this discussion. Cooper hesitated, not sure what to do. Alvix blew him a kiss.

"Just go and get everything ready for our visitors. I'll be fine."

"We'll be back in a little bit and discuss the arrangements we made."

"Okay."

He listened to them walk out to the front of the house where the communications/security room had been built. When he heard the door shut, he smiled sadly and finished cleaning off the table.

Alvix rinsed the dishes before setting them in the dishwasher. He'd been surprised at how primitive things were on Earth when they arrived, yet he found he liked the busy work involved with making meals and putting things away. It kept his hands busy while his mind got to wander.

Staring out the window at the back yard, he braced his hands against the counter and laughed. Who would have thought he'd come to the point of sacrificing himself again? Yet he had no choice because he wasn't willing to let these men risk their lives for him. Not after everything they'd gone through.

There were a hundred ways he could save himself and he would, but not before forcing the GalMil to make some concessions. He'd make sure his friends were safe from retribution. Blinking slowly, his mind skated over his options and he plotted out the different ways he could go about surrendering himself to the GalMil agents sent to retrieve him.

CHAPTER 20

The villagers were warned and the perimeter taken care of by his men and a few of the villagers who chose to fight with them instead of going into hiding. Cooper didn't look down on the ones who hid. They had children and loved ones to take care of. Hell, that's what he was doing. Protecting Alvix and he was ready to die if he had to.

Rivers stood next to him as they watched the GalMil ships land several klicks down the road. It would be an hour or so before they approached the house. They had lookouts stationed all down the road who would alert them when the soldiers headed out.

"This is it, Coop."

He glanced at his best friend and nodded. "We'll make our stand here. We can prove to them that coming after us will cost them more than they're willing to throw at us."

"If we don't all die first."

"Always the optimist, my friend." He grinned and punched Rivers in the arm. "So where did you put everyone?"

"Steele and Pope are with half our villagers guarding the back trails. Apple and Callum have the sides with various villagers. You and I will take the front. You've been voted our spokesman."

"Why?"

"Because you're the highest ranking officer." Rivers winked.

"Great. I thought I got out of that when we separated," he grumbled.

Rivers laughed. "Did you really think any of us wanted the job? You're going to be our leader until we all die."

He wasn't sure he wanted to know that. Taking responsibility while in the military was one thing. Being in charge now that they were civilians seemed strange.

"Don't worry about it. All it really means is that you're wearing a target on your chest. They'll take you out first, hoping we'll panic when we don't have you around to tell us what to do."

"That's great. Thanks, Rivers."

"No problem."

The red light lit up on the console, and he snatched up his rifle from where it rested against the wall.

"They're on the move." He headed out of the communications room toward the back of the house. "Where's Alvix?"

Rivers glanced around before shrugging. "I'm not sure. I haven't seen him since we handed out the assignments. He's around here somewhere."

Cooper nodded, but his stomach clenched. Something was going to happen and he was afraid Alvix might have plans he hadn't discussed with Cooper.

"Coop, you better get your ass out here." Callum's yell reached them as they opened the front door.

"What the fuck?" Cooper's mouth dropped open.

Alvix stood at the end of the lane, facing the squad of twenty GalMil soldiers.

"Alvix, what the hell are you doing?" He managed to grit out between his clenched teeth. Gesturing to Rivers, he started down the front steps toward Alvix.

"Stop where you are, Cooper. I'll take care of this." Alvix held up his hand and a small stream of fire streamed from it to create barrier between Alvix and Cooper.

"You're going to get yourself killed or captured. If you don't, then I'll kill you when I get my hands on you." He gripped his rifle tight and jumped through the fire barrier. The metal covering him flamed white hot, but cooled immediately after he was through.

Alvix shot him an irritated look. "You just can't stop trying to save me."

Cooper stared at Alvix. "You're joking, right? Last time I saved your ass was because you took our place with some sort of crazy flame creature. This time, I'm trying to keep you from being turned into a lab rat."

"I told you I can take care of myself."

One of the GalMil soldiers raised his gun, but before Cooper could do anything about it, Alvix waved a hand in the man's direction and his weapon melted into a pile of metal. The soldier yelped and jumped back. The other squad members shifted uneasily, but held their ground.

"Since when can you do that?" Cooper tilted his head in the direction of the liquid metal.

Alvix wrinkled his nose while he thought. "I've always been able to do that, but I've never had any reason to do it before. It's too easy to let the fire get hold of me and let it burn."

"Cooper, I demand you turn over the fire-eater known as Alvix to my custody."

Cooper frowned as he turned to find Fulcher standing behind the first line of men. "I should've known you'd be involved in some way."

Lieutenant Fulcher smirked. "I was more than happy to take this mission. You've gotten away with insubordination because of preferential treatment from a certain general. I'm happy to say that issue is being rectified as we speak."

"Oh, you think so? Well, we'll see how long the general stays under GalMil guard. You might be surprised." Cooper folded his arms over his chest, keeping his rifle pointed down. He didn't want any of the men facing him to think he was aiming at them.

Fulcher's smile was more like a grimace. "Yes, we'll see. I don't think Supreme General Gateway's rich friends will get him out this time. Now give that one over to me and I'll let you live."

Alvix shook his head. "Somehow, I doubt that. I think you'll order your men to kill Cooper and his men after you have me in custody. You'll make up some story about how they tried to rescue me and your men were forced to use extreme measures to stop them."

Surprise flashed on Fulcher's face, and Cooper realized that Alvix had been telling the truth. Fulcher didn't plan to leave any of them alive. "Are you a mind reader now?" he whispered to Alvix.

His lover shook his head. "No, just know the type of guy this Fulcher is and he's not the type to play fair or be honest with anyone. He's all about what's right for him. He'd turn on his grandmother to get ahead in the universe."

Alvix's voice carried, and Fulcher turned beet red.

"That really isn't an attractive color on you," Alvix commented, rubbing the palms of his hands on his thighs.

"Shut up. You're not even human. You're just some scientist's experiment gone wrong." Fulcher's words flew from his lips like daggers.

"Which one of us? The metal man next to me, or am I the rogue experiment?"

Cooper wondered the same thing.

"You." Fulcher pointed at Alvix. "Though Cooper and his men aren't much better."

"Well, so much for being born from a star," Alvix muttered with a hint of laughter.

"Not sure I believed that anyway," said Cooper.

They grinned at each other, and Fulcher's frustration seemed to mount.

"I think we're pissing him off." Alvix tilted his head towards the lieutenant.

"I think you're right. Why is that?" Cooper wanted to move to stand in front of Alvix to protect him from any random bullet or laser shot. Yet his lover wouldn't appreciate the protection.

"Because we're not giving him the respect he thinks he deserves."

Cooper spied a man edging toward the side to try to flank them. Cooper's gaze darted to the man and back at Alvix. Alvix's eyebrows shot up before he made a slight gesture with one hand and flames rose, herding the man back to the others.

Alvix swung around, but not before Cooper saw the anger burning in Alvix's eyes. Fire burst from the ground, even where there wasn't anything to burn. The weapons Fulcher's men held melted and they dropped back until there was no one between Fulcher and Alvix. Cooper stayed with Alvix as the man stalked closer to Fulcher.

"Where are you going, you cowards? I'll have all of you brought up on dereliction of duty or insubordination." Spit flew from Fulcher's lips as he screamed at his men.

The laugh emerging from Alvix's mouth chilled even Cooper to the core. He looked over at Alvix and took a step to the side. Orange sparks danced through the man's blond hair, giving a strange living look to it. The air around Alvix crackled and Cooper could feel his skin heating.

"They might have to follow you, Fulcher, but when it seems that their superior officer has lost his fucking mind, they can choose not to obey orders." Alvix pushed into Fulcher's personal space. "They're the smart ones."

Sweat beaded on Fulcher's face, dripping down his chin to hit the ground. Fulcher's gaze skipped over to Cooper before focusing on Alvix again.

"You'll have the full might of the GalMil after you if you do anything to me," Fulcher warned.

Alvix snorted and reached out. Cooper wanted to ask what Alvix was doing, but didn't think he really wanted to know. Abject terror roiled in Fulcher's eyes as Alvix's fingers drew closer to his chest. The lieutenant's hands twitched like he wanted to knock Alvix away, but couldn't bring himself to risk getting burned by him.

Cooper flinched as Alvix pressed his hand to the armor covering Fulcher's chest. Whatever was going to happen wouldn't be pretty.

"This armor isn't fire-proof, is it?"

"Alvix, what are you doing?" Worry compelled Cooper to ask. "Fulcher's right. If we do anything to him, the GalMil will come after us with everything they've got. Right now, I think it's just a small group of military men interested in us. If we attack a GalMil officer, the others will be forced to retaliate."

"I don't plan on killing him."

"If you aren't going to kill him, what are you doing?" He clenched his hands to keep from knocking Alvix's hand from Fulcher, unsure whether he wanted to save Fulcher or keep Alvix from being contaminated by touching the man.

Alvix bared his teeth in a snarl. "I'm going to leave him with a warning. He can go tell his superiors as well."

The scent of burning fabric and metal filled the air, giving Cooper an idea of what Alvix was doing. Glancing over his shoulder, he saw Rivers standing on the front steps of the house.

::*What should I do?*::

::*Stop him, I guess.*:: Rivers didn't sound very convincing.

::*I'm getting the feeling you think I should let Alvix continue what he's doing.*::

::*He's not hurting us, and it could be a very effective warning for GalMil to stay away from us.*:: Steele jumped in.

A strangled scream interrupted the silent conversation, drawing Cooper's attention back to the scene in front of him. Smoke rose from the armor Fulcher wore, and Cooper saw a sliver of white flesh exposed by the burnt shirt. Blood trickled from Fulcher's lip where the man had bitten it. Cooper gagged as the smell of cooking flesh filled the air.

::*One of us should really stop this.*:: Callum didn't sound any more convinced than the others.

::*Let's face it. None of us want to save the s.o.b., but can you trust Flame to do what he said and not kill the bastard?*:: Rivers shifted where he stood several feet away from them.

Cooper studied the man next to him. What Alvix was doing scared him deep inside, yet he did believe Alvix wasn't trying to kill Fulcher. Who could say that the way Alvix dealt with the situation wouldn't end up saving them in the end?

::Yes, I trust him. I don't know what he's doing, but I don't think he wants to kill Fulcher, though if he did, I wouldn't blame him.::

::Then we stay quiet and let Flame take care of this for us.:: Pope's statement brought agreement from the others.

"Help me," Fulcher croaked, trying to grab Cooper's arm.

The pain in the lieutenant's face almost broke Cooper's resolve, but before he could call Alvix off, his lover removed his hand, leaving a wicked looking print on Fulcher's chest. Fulcher dropped to his knees, gasping and sobbing.

"Come get him and go back to your ship," Alvix ordered the soldiers standing a few feet away.

They stared at Cooper, who nodded and gestured for them to come forward. The two bravest raced up, grabbed Fulcher under the arms and started dragging him back.

"Wait."

They froze, and Cooper tensed, holding his breath to see what Alvix was going to do. Alvix stalked over to the drooping Fulcher and lifted his chin so their eyes met. Fulcher's eyes widened with fear and he flinched away from Alvix's touch. Alvix's cold smile chilled Cooper.

"Tell your superiors that if anyone comes after us, I will burn everyone who threatens me and my friends. After that, I will come to GalMil headquarters, torch the place and everyone who's there." Alvix crouched closer to Fulcher, his gaze narrowed and cruel. "I'm not joking about this either. Show them what I did to you and warn them that their punishment will be much worse."

Alvix dropped Fulcher's chin and spun around. The confidence in that move told Cooper all he needed to know. Alvix believed he could deal with whatever the GalMil sent and the thought of Alvix having that much power intrigued Cooper, as well as frightening him slightly. What could happen if Alvix lost control of the fire? Could Alvix get it under his grip or would he burn himself out? Cooper nodded to Fulcher's men to go.

::Pope and I will follow them, Coop.:: Apple informed him.

::Good. Just be careful and report back as soon as you know they've left.::

::Will do.:: Apple sent him a mental salute.

Cooper waited until the squadron of soldiers disappeared around the bend before turning and heading back into the house. Rivers and Steele were already in the living room, one standing by the window and the other leaning on the fireplace. Both stared at Alvix, who sprawled in one of the chairs, his legs flung over the arm.

Resting his rifle against the wall, Cooper considered what to say. He glanced over at his men, and Rivers shrugged. Steele's grin told Cooper the man got a kick out of Alvix's actions.

"Where's Callum?" he asked, buying some time to organize his thoughts.

"He's sending the villagers home, telling them the threat is over for now." Rivers scrubbed a trembling hand over his mouth.

"Is it?" Cooper met Alvix's steady gaze.

"Is what?" Alvix frowned.

"Is the threat over?"

*   *   *

Shrugging, Alvix went back to staring at the ceiling. "Like Rivers said, the threat is over for now. It depends whether or not the higher-ups in the GalMil believe I'll do what I said I'd do."

He heard Cooper move closer to him and heaved a silent sigh. He really didn't want to talk about any of the shit that had happened outside.

"Did you know about the experiments?"

Cooper's question was low, and Alvix shifted, dropping his feet to the floor and bracing his elbows on his knees. He studied the hardwood floor's grain as he thought about what to tell Cooper.

"Alvix?"

"Yes, I did know the people who raised me were part of a GalMil experiment that went wrong somewhere along the way." He shrugged and looked up, meeting Cooper's gaze.

"Why did you tell me that bullshit about being a star?"

Pushing to his feet, Alvix paused for a second before pacing in front of the others. He tucked his hands in his front pockets and hunched forward. "What does it matter how I became what I am? Whether I was born or made. It doesn't matter, and to tell you the truth, I don't know. I don't know if I was part of the original experiment or if I was born after the others escaped."

"No wonder the scientists want to get hold of you. If you were born outside the lab, it means your powers can be passed on to your children." Steele edged away from the window. "Were there more children in your group?"

He shook his head. "Not in mine. I don't know if there were others hidden on different planets or anything like that. We tried to stay in the shadows, not wanting to bring attention to ourselves. That's why I learned to have such tight control over my power. No point in hiding when one moment of fear or anger could light me up like a meteor shower."

"The scientists really have no moral or ethical boundaries, do they?" Callum stalked in. "I mean look what they did to us."

"Oh, I'm sure there are some who help people, just not try to see who can come up with the strangest creations." Rivers slumped onto the couch, where Callum joined him.

Alvix noticed how they sat as close as they could to each other, arms and legs touching. Steele sat in one of the chairs.

"Did you mean what you told Fulcher?"

Alvix stopped and looked at Cooper. "Yes, I was serious. If GalMil sends more troops here to take us in, I'll burn them to the ground. Then I will go to GalMil headquarters and tear the place apart. I'm done being a victim and hiding what I am. They will reap what they've sown."

Instead of looking scared by his statement, the others nodded. Cooper frowned slightly, but didn't say anything.

"Listen, I don't know how I came to be and it doesn't matter whether it's from a star or a lab. I exist and I have this power. No more trying to blend in." He held up a hand to stop Cooper when the man opened his mouth. "I'm not saying I'm going to take on the GalMil. I don't believe in their policies, but it's not my place to change them. I'm just not going to back down when they challenge me. Fire will keep me free, and you as well, if you choose to stay with me."

Cooper strolled over to him and stood right in front of him, studying him. "You're staying here?"

He shrugged. "Why not? I own this place now. I think I'll hole up here for a little while, figure out what I want to do. I don't really need to be a transport pilot anymore since I have money, but I'm not the kind of guy who likes to sit around doing nothing."

"None of us is." Callum spoke up.

"True. We'll have to talk about our future in the next couple of days."

"The GalMil ship is gone." Apple returned with Pope.

"Do you think we'll hear from them about this whole thing?" Alvix glanced from Cooper to the other men.

Pope rested his ass on the arm of Steele's chair, while Apple joined Callum and Rivers on the couch. They all shook their heads.

"I think the only answer we'll get from them is silence. They'll ignore us." Cooper rested his hand at the small of Alvix's back.

"What about Pope's father?" He looked at Pope.

Grimacing, Pope shrugged. "I guess we can only hope his friends are as powerful as we think."

Alvix didn't offer platitudes. Pope knew the score. If the GalMil wanted to, they could make General Gateway disappear and there wouldn't be anything Pope could do.

Cooper broke the silence. "Come on. We need to take stock of what we have and what we'll need to go to the closest city for."

His men stood and wandered out of the living room, talking amongst themselves. Alvix swayed and sighed as Cooper pulled him tight against his chest. The cool metal making up Cooper's skin soothed the burn inside Alvix.

"You're burning up, honey," Cooper murmured, his lips brushing Alvix's temple.

"The fire comes at a cost. It raises my internal temperature, plus it drains my energy. Not as badly as it used to when we first landed here. I've learned how to harness it. I really hope they'll leave us alone. I don't relish having to fry everything or anyone that they send."

"Even though they probably spent a lot of money on my unit, investing in the titanium skin and all, I think the risk isn't worth the reward. They can make more of us in their labs." Cooper slid his hands up under Alvix's shirt, running them up and down his back.

"True," he muttered and nuzzled under Cooper's chin.

"Are you two coming or are you just going to cuddle in the living room the rest of the day?" Callum yelled from the hallway.

"I think cuddling sounds good," Alvix yelled back, but he stepped away from Cooper. "Why don't you go give those guys some directions? I'm going to lie down for a little while. A nap usually perks me up and settles the flames for a time."

Cooper cradled Alvix's face and smiled. "Okay. If you need me, though, just call. I'll be happy to help put the fire out."

Alvix laughed. "Having you around doesn't help my temperature at all. You make me hotter than if I flew my ship into one of the many suns in the universe."

"Good to hear that." Cooper winked before spinning Alvix around and slapping him on the ass. "Now go get some rest. I'll grab you for dinner."

He strolled up the stairs, tension draining from him like someone had pulled a plug and it was emptying out of his body. By the time he got to his room, he was staggering, drunk on exhaustion and the loss of adrenaline. His clothes landed in a pile on the floor, along with his boots, and he dropped face first onto the mattress, having only enough energy to wrap himself up in a blanket before passing out.

EPILOGUE

Alvix looked up as Callum skidded into the room with Rivers only a step behind him.

"Where's Pope?"

Shrugging, Alvix leaned back in his chair and stretched. "I'm not sure. Cooper took him and Steele out to look at the ships to get them outfitted with the right supplies for the transport runs. Why?"

"We're going to be getting a couple visitors soon. Actually, they're on their way and should be arriving tomorrow."

Callum's infectious happiness brought a grin to Alvix's face.

"Supreme General Gateway's finally free?"

"Yep. Jensen sent us a communication a few minutes ago. She procured Gateway's release and they're on their way here." Callum flapped a sheet of paper in Alvix's face.

He grabbed it and set it on the desk, but didn't look at it. "What were the conditions?"

"He had to resign and turn over control of Tative to the GalMil."

"Ouch." He winced. "That one had to hurt."

"Probably, but I think it's a small price to pay. He could've been stuck in prison for years and a GalMil prison is no place for a supreme general."

"True." He handed the paper to Rivers. "Go find Pope and give him the good news."

Rivers nodded. "We'll catch you at lunch."

Alvix laughed as Callum and Rivers shot out of the room, Callum pestering Rivers to allow him to be the one who told Pope. Standing, he twisted and popped his spine, releasing the stiffness from his neck and back that came from hunching over the books all day.

He wandered over to one of the windows that overlooked the backyard of his house. Acres of rolling green greeted his gaze and he smiled. Who would have imagined he'd own a place like this on Earth where only the rich came to play? Yet he did own this place and a very successful transport company. There was enough money coming in that he didn't have to fly one of his ships unless he wanted to. Every so often, he'd go out on a run, just to keep his fingers on the pulse of his business.

Through Gateway's contacts, they'd discovered the GalMil had declared Alvix, Cooper and the others immune to GalMil retribution. Guess someone believed that Alvix's threats were real. They'd also found out that what Fulcher had said was the truth. Alvix's parents were part of a GalMil experiment. The whole group of people Alvix lived with had started out as GalMil prisoners until they managed to escape from the labs. That's why they suppressed their power and hid from society, though the GalMil recaptured most of them throughout the years. Alvix was the only one left free, and the higher-ups in the GalMil didn't seem inclined to come after him.

Cooper strolled into Alvix's line of vision and looked up at the window where Alvix stood. Winking, Cooper blew him a kiss. Alvix rested his hand on the glass in response. How strange was it that he loved a man covered in titanium? A man who smelled of metal, musk, and oil most of the time. Yet Cooper was exactly what Alvix needed when the fire got too hot. They fit together in so many ways.

Each was a misfit in his own way, but together they were perfect for each other. They loved each other, though they rarely said the words. Each action and gesture spoke of their love without needing to utter it out loud.

Alvix gestured for Cooper to come in. His lover grinned knowingly. As Cooper disappeared around the corner of the house, Alvix headed upstairs to his room. So much had happened in the year since they first met that it was nice to have the leisure to spend time with Cooper without worrying about someone attacking them.

He stripped and sprawled naked on the bed, idly stroking his cock while he waited for Cooper to join him, letting the sexual fire build and simmer, knowing Cooper would be there soon to soothe the burn.

.

T. A. CHASE

T. A. Chase lives a life without boundaries. Being fascinated by life and how different we all are, he writes about the things that make us unique. He finds beauty in all kinds of love and enjoys sharing those insights. He lives in the Midwest with his partner of twelve years. When he isn't writing, he's watching movies, reading and living life to the fullest.

*　　*　　*

**Don't miss *Nowhere Diner: Finding Love*
by T. A.Chase,
available at AmberQuill.com!**

Leaving Minnesota, Timothy Gapin doesn't have any plans except getting as far away from all the memories as he can before his money runs out. His secret lover has married, breaking his heart and making him chose a life in the open rather than a relationship built on lies.

Little does Tim know that four days later he would grab dinner at a diner and find a place to stop. Somehow this diner in the middle of nowhere becomes his home and the people who work there his family. In addition to the workers at the diner, Tim meets Bernie Capley, a long-haul trucker who isn't all he seems to be.

Falling in love with Bernie is easy for Tim, but the past has a way of barging into the present, forcing decisions that affect their future...

AMBER QUILL PRESS, LLC
THE GOLD STANDARD IN PUBLISHING

QUALITY BOOKS
IN BOTH PRINT AND ELECTRONIC FORMATS

ACTION/ADVENTURE	SUSPENSE/THRILLER
SCIENCE FICTION	DARK FANTASY
MAINSTREAM	ROMANCE
HORROR	EROTICA
FANTASY	GLBT
WESTERN	MYSTERY
PARANORMAL	HISTORICAL
YOUNG ADULT	NON-FICTION

AMBER QUILL PRESS, LLC
http://www.amberquill.com